She studied him for a second and he glanced at her. "Something wrong?"

"No, nothing. I've just never met...well, someone like you before."

"Someone like me," he mused. "What does that mean?"

"You're a cowboy."

He flashed her a smile. "What gave it away? The hat, the boots, the saddle in the back, or maybe it's the subtle whiff of cow lingering in the air?"

"All of the above," she said, but her voice revealed she knew he was teasing her. "Of course, in my line of work it pays to be observant."

"And I bet you d̶o̶n̶'̶t̶ ̶m̶i̶s̶s̶ ̶m̶u̶c̶h̶."

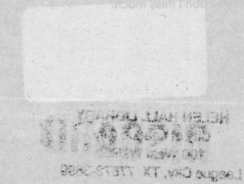

COWBOY SECRETS

ALICE SHARPE

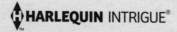

HARLEQUIN INTRIGUE®

This book is dedicated with love to Amalia Anina Mauro LeVelle

Recycling programs
for this product may
not exist in your area.

ISBN-13: 978-0-373-69919-3

Cowboy Secrets

Copyright © 2016 by Alice Sharpe

This edition published by arrangement with Harlequin Books S.A.

For questions and comments about the quality of this book, please contact us at CustomerService@Harlequin.com.

HARLEQUIN®
www.Harlequin.com

Printed in U.S.A.

Alice Sharpe met her husband-to-be on a cold, foggy beach in Northern California. Their union has survived the rearing of two children, a handful of earthquakes, numerous cats and a few special dogs, the latest of which is a yellow Lab named Annie Rose. Alice and her husband now live in a small rural town in Oregon, where she devotes the majority of her time to pursuing her second love, writing. You can write to her c/o Harlequin Books, 233 Broadway, Suite 1001, New York, NY 10279. An SASE for reply is appreciated.

Books by Alice Sharpe

Harlequin Intrigue

The Brothers of Hastings Ridge Ranch
Cowboy Incognito
Cowboy Undercover
Cowboy Secrets

The Rescuers
Shattered
Stranded

The Legacy
Undercover Memories
Montana Refuge
Soldier's Redemption

Open Sky Ranch
Westin's Wyoming
Westin's Legacy
Westin Family Ties

Visit the Author Profile page at Harlequin.com for more titles.

CAST OF CHARACTERS

Pike Hastings—The world of this sexy, thoughtful cowboy—whose deep roots cling to the soil and the people of Hastings Ridge—is thrown into a tailspin with the arrivals of his stepsister and the fascinating big-city PI with the flaming-red hair. The trick will be keeping both of them alive.

Sierra Hyde—When the summons to Idaho tears her away from a tedious divorce investigation, she's almost relieved. That respite quickly fades as she faces her sister's vivid terror. Is it imaginary or as real as the thundering awareness zinging between her and Pike?

Tess Foster—Related to both Pike and Sierra, she claims she's just witnessed her boyfriend's cold-blooded murder; she's positive she's in line to become the next victim.

Danny Cooke—Tess's boyfriend whose cold-blooded death she saw with her own eyes. Or did she?

Raoul Ruiz—Danny's drug dealer and the last man known to have seen him.

Rolland Bean—He was Sierra's deceased father's friend and adviser. As the situation grows increasingly complicated, she looks to him for sound advice.

Anthony Bean—Rolland's son. He's just as creepy as he was when they were both kids.

Savannah Papadakis—Sierra's wealthy, reclusive client has a straying husband. Her disappearance opens a whole new can of worms.

Spiro Papadakis—How far will Savannah's estranged husband go to keep his wife's fortune?

Giselle Montgomery—The call girl with whom it appears Spiro conducted an affair. Her violent murder is fodder for the tabloids—but does it affect the continuing danger to Tess?

Chapter One

Sierra Hyde yawned into her fist as she nursed a glass of white wine at a long mahogany bar. The music, the booths on the back wall and the big mirror behind the bottles all reeked of familiarity.

Her main interest, however, wasn't the establishment, but the solitary woman sitting alone at a dark booth near the back of the room. Her name was Natalia Bonaparte, age thirty-three. Occupation: job counselor. Frequent glances at the diamond watch sparkling on her wrist suggested whomever she was waiting to meet was late, but Sierra already knew this. Her job was to catch a photo of the man who joined the woman. According to Sierra's client, Savannah Papadakis, that man was going to be Savannah's estranged husband.

Yeah, well, it better be him because trailing Natalia was getting tedious and it had only been two days. The woman had a pretty active after-hour party life.

"Will you have another?" the bartender asked as he ran a rag along the bar. Sierra looked down at her glass and realized she'd imbibed half the wine.

"I'll have a ginger ale this time," she said. With any luck, her client's husband would show up, she'd get a few photos and be on her way back to New York City within the next few minutes. She needed a good night's sleep after the disco stakeout last night.

He left to pour her drink right as the door opened. Sierra darted a quick glance. Two young guys barely old enough to legally walk through the door held each other up as they staggered to the bar and plopped down on either side of Sierra.

"Hey, pretty lady," one of them said. The guy's breath reached her nose before his words reached her ears and she instinctively flinched.

The bartender showed up with the ginger ale and took orders for two beers, while Sierra declined to let her new "friends" buy her one, too. The door opened again, sending a renewed jolt of cold January air into the bar. A man about the right age sauntered in. His perfectly groomed head of white hair caught every stray beam of light as he looked from the bar to the tables, past groups of revelers, until his gaze stopped on the far corner where Sierra knew the blonde sat. He seemed to momentarily frown before crossing the room to join her. The woman greeted him by lifting one of her hands, which he kissed. Sierra witnessed all this by watching their hazy reflections in the mirror that backed the bar.

The two drunks were both leaning closer to her, making her thankful she hadn't taken off her jacket. She had to get rid of them if she was going to get the pictures and escape this place.

"Those gals over there are giving you the eye," she whispered to the one on her left. She nodded at a table a good distance away, where two women pushing forty sat talking over martini glasses. As far as Sierra knew, neither one was even aware the guys at the bar existed.

"Them?" the one on Sierra's left said after turning to stare.

"Too old," the man on her right said. "Besides, they ain't looking at us."

"Sure they are," she said as she took a pair of tortoiseshell glasses out of her pocket and slipped them on her face. "They just look away whenever one of you turns around."

"You know, dude, there's nothing wrong with bagging a couple of cougars," the other guy said with a speculative note in his voice.

"But we can't abandon this little gal," the one on the right insisted.

"Sure you can," Sierra said. "I'm about to leave, anyway."

He grinned and cracked his knuckles. "That case, I call dibs on the brunette."

Both men wobbled their way toward their new targets. Heaving a sigh of relief, Sierra once again focused on the mirror's reflection. The lighting in that booth sucked. Details were hard to see.

She turned casually on her stool, glanced at the two women, who had apparently invited the drunks to sit down with them, and looked at the blonde's table as she activated the camera hidden in the nose bridge of the frames of her glasses. She counted out a dozen shots, then got to her feet, put a twenty on the bar and made her way to the restroom, which meant she walked right past the booth. To her relief, the candlelight on their table was adequate at close range, and she took several pictures while passing, mostly of the woman, though the point was to get them both in the frame.

After washing her hands, Sierra retraced her steps, this time angling for a better shot of her two subjects. As she snapped a photo, the man called the bartender over. She darted him a startled glance. He looked right through her and she continued walking. She'd been so sure! But that accent…

Spiro Papadakis had been in the States for over a decade, but according to his wife, his Greek accent was still pronounced. This man sounded like the Jersey shore. He looked up at her as she passed and their eyes met. He blinked and looked away. She'd seen several photographs of her target and there was something familiar about this guy despite the voice.

Well, she'd download and study the pictures later. For now, her job here was done and she walked outside. Freezing rain pelted her face as she made her way to her car. Her phone chirped but she didn't recognize the caller ID and answered cautiously. "Yes?"

"Is this Sierra Hyde?"

"Yes," Sierra said as a sound from behind caused her to glance over her shoulder. She'd been a PI for almost five years now and liked to think her instincts picked up anything unusual in her environment. For a heartbeat she studied the facade. The lake behind the tavern was huge and black, and sent a layer of mist swirling around the painted wooden fish over the door. There didn't appear to be anyone else around.

She turned her attention back to her caller. "Who is this?" she asked as she traversed the crowded lot to the very back corner, where she'd parked.

"My name is Pike Hastings," a male voice said. "I'm sort of related to your sister, Tess."

"I know who you are," she said as she spotted the bright red bumper sticker promoting her choice of candidate for the upcoming mayoral election. She beeped the car open and settled behind the wheel. "You're Mona's son."

"That's right. I know we've never met—"

"Oh, my gosh, are you calling about Tess?" Sierra interrupted as she closed the car door behind her. "Has my little sister shown up? Does her dad know? Is she okay?"

"Yes, no, hard to say. Yes, she showed up, but here at my place. One minute she says call her dad, the next she refuses to let me do it. I'm not sure how she is except for a head cold and what looks to me like a major case of the jitters."

"You're in Montana, right?"

"No, the family ranch is in Idaho. About Tess, like I said, something has her spooked but she insists on talking to you and me together. Can you come right away?"

"Of course," Sierra said.

"That's great," he said, and there was no missing the relief in his voice. "I took the liberty of buying you a plane ticket. I'll email it to you. The only flight I could get you on leaves at five tomorrow morning from New York, I hope that's okay."

Sierra suppressed a groan. There went the night's sleep she'd been hoping for. On the other hand, Tess had been mostly out of touch since a couple of weeks before Halloween. Sierra was so relieved to hear she was alive and breathing—even if it was in Idaho— that she would have walked there if she'd had to.

"I'll pick you up at the airport," he added.

"That isn't necessary," she assured him. "I'll rent a car."

"I insist," he said. "The ranch can be hard to find and the roads are kind of tricky this time of year and your phone might not work," he told her. "We don't exactly have the same cell coverage you're used to. Trust me on this."

"Okay," she said, and added her thanks before clicking off. Almost immediately, a sound outside the window made her look up and she gasped. It took her a second to make out the squished-up features of one of the drunks from the bar.

"Hey, baby, you're voting for the wrong guy," he said with a wide sweep of his arm toward the back of her car. "Jakes is a loser. Vote Yardley!"

She smiled and nodded and hit the door lock. No way was she rolling down the window. She started the car and hoped she didn't back over one of his feet.

"Hey, come on back inside!" he squawked and reeled away. Did that comment about the mayoral candidates for New York City mean he had to drive all the way back to the city tonight? She sincerely hoped the bartender confiscated his keys and called him a cab.

Jumpy now, her mind racing with everything she had to do in the next seven hours, she drove out of the parking lot and headed home. A glance in the rearview mirror reassured her no one followed.

It crossed her mind that she didn't know why it had even occurred to her to check.

PIKE HASTINGS WAS glad the predicted winter storm hadn't materialized...yet. He arrived at the airport in Boise a half hour before Sierra's flight was due to land and made the loop, keeping an eye out for a woman who fit her description. He'd never met her, had never even seen a picture of her. She shared only a mother with Tess, and Tess had warned him that while she had inherited her mother's genes, Sierra had not. She'd told him only to look for a tall woman with red hair and an attitude.

As descriptions went, it wasn't a lot to go on, but he figured they'd find each other without too much trouble. He eventually parked in the loading zone in front of the airline on which he'd booked her flight and got out of the SUV. Within minutes, a woman headed out of the building pulling a carry-on, impatience written all over her face.

But what a face. One in a million women could

claim skin like hers: creamy, glowing, perfect. Large green eyes the color of spring ivy might look frustrated right now, but there was nothing wrong with their shape, just as her lips formed a lovely curve and her auburn hair fell in a glistening sheet to frame her jaw. She wore a black suede jacket and matching riding boots, skintight black jeans and a white shirt. A brilliant solitaire diamond glistened at her throat and a large leather handbag that could double as a saddlebag hung over one shoulder.

A large man with a mustache walked behind her. He wore a baseball cap pulled down over his eyes, but Pike could see that he was staring at Sierra's seductive shape just as intently as Pike had. The man seemed to become aware of Pike's gaze and he put his hand up to his eyes and veered away as though embarrassed to be caught staring. Pike could have assured him just about any man would have ogled a bit.

"Sierra Hyde?" Pike said, stepping forward. She turned as though just becoming aware of him, pocketed her phone and maintained eye contact as Pike approached. He tried to see himself through her eyes and wondered what conclusions she might be making about him. He could only hope they were as flattering as the ones he'd drawn about her.

"You must be Pike," she said, holding out her hand and shaking his with a firm, no-nonsense grip. "My phone works," she added.

"Wait until we get out in the middle of nowhere," he said with a smile.

"No doubt. Funny how dependent we get on our gadgets."

Tess had said her sister was a private eye and he bet she was good at what she did. She didn't look as though she'd tolerate being anything but good.

"Let me help you with that," he said, reaching for her suitcase. "Please, go ahead and take a seat."

She seemed almost reluctant to let him help, but did as he asked. He deposited the suitcase in the back of the SUV as she climbed into the passenger seat. "Did you have a nice flight?" he asked as he pulled away from the curb. She had turned to look back at the terminal and took a second to look forward again. Was there something back there? He glanced into his rearview mirror and saw nothing but a sea of cars. "Is everything okay?" he asked.

"Yes," she said, avoiding eye contact. "And my flight was fine. How is Tess?"

"Pretty miserable," he said.

"Has she told you anything?"

"No. But I was referring to her head cold as well as her emotional state."

"She hasn't even said where she went after she left home all of a sudden?"

"Not a thing. I only heard from her once in all that time and that was right before Christmas. She texted me but never responded when I texted her back."

"That's about the same thing that happened to me, too," Sierra said. "But I'm surprised she tuned you out. I know you've done your best to visit her

every few months and get along with her dad. She
even came out to your ranch once or twice, right?"

"Yes. And I've flown to LA. She's a nice kid who
seemed to get lost in the shuffle."

Sierra nodded, the assessing look back in her eyes.
"Frankly, I'm surprised she wants me to come at all.
She's been angry with me for years."

"I wouldn't take it personally. She's just kind of
confused. And I, for one, am very glad you're here,"
he added. "I can tell she's scared of something, but
she insists she wants to talk to both of us. I was hoping you two had made some inroads with each other."

"I wanted her to come stay in New York with me
after our mom died," Sierra said, "but Doug was her
legal guardian and he insisted she stay with him in
LA. There wasn't much I could do about it. I think
Tess thought I didn't want her. And I don't know…
I was about eighteen at the time and she was what,
six or seven? I'd seen little of her since before she
started kindergarten. I tried to stay in touch but after
her dad hooked up with that woman—" She paused
and cast him a quick look. "Sorry, I forgot for a second that Mona is your mother."

"I'm under no illusions when it comes to my
mother," he assured her. "She left about five minutes after I was born and never looked back. Don't
worry about offending me."

"Well, in that case, let's just say Mona got caught
up in what was left of Doug's Hollywood glamour.
She didn't want Tess around, or me, either, for that
matter. Unfortunately, Doug is about as perceptive

as a cantaloupe. Tess was problematic and he dealt with it by ignoring her. Those two people are hopeless as parents, but I'm still surprised that they didn't do more to find her when she walked out in October."

"Mom said that Tess stormed off in that car Doug bought her. She was eighteen, legally an adult. I think it was easier for both Mom and Doug to throw up their hands. And you have to remember this was right after Mona caught good old Doug fooling around at his restaurant and kicked him out. When Tess left the next day I think Mona said good riddance to both of them." He shook his head. "People, right? Give me a horse any day."

She studied him for a second and he glanced at her. "Something wrong?"

"No, nothing. I've just never met...well, someone like you before."

"Someone like me," he mused. "What does that mean?"

"You're a cowboy."

He flashed her a smile. "What gave it away? The hat, the boots, the saddle in the back? Or maybe it's the subtle whiff of cow lingering in the air?"

"All of the above," she said, but her voice revealed she knew he was teasing her. "Of course, in my line of work it pays to be observant."

"And I bet you don't miss much."

"I'm not sure if I do or not. Exactly how far into the middle of nowhere is your ranch located?" she added as they left the Boise city limits.

"About two hours north of here." He was aware of her disappointment upon hearing that. "Listen, there's not all that much to see between here and there," he added. "Why don't you close your eyes for a while so you'll be fresh when we get there?"

"I couldn't do that," she said.

"Why not?"

She shrugged lovely shoulders. The gesture seemed out of character for her, like a tiny little beachhead of uncertainty. "It would seem, I don't know, too familiar, I guess."

"Don't worry. If you snore I won't tell a soul."

"I do not snore," she said.

He smiled at her. "Go ahead. Close your eyes. I'll turn on the radio so I can't hear any little snorts or grunts—"

"I don't snort or grunt, either," she said, but this time she laughed. "Okay, I'll try to get a little sleep. My eyes feel like sandpaper. Wake me up before we're actually there, okay? I'd like to orient myself."

"Sure thing." He fiddled with the FM station until he found easy listening music that shouldn't keep her awake, but realized almost instantly it would take a brass marching band to accomplish that. One second she was sitting kind of stiffly in her seat, tilted cautiously toward the window, and the next her head had rolled forward until her chin touched her collarbone. She didn't look all that comfortable, but he resisted the urge to shift her. Something told him she was not the kind of woman to touch, even innocently, while she slept.

SIERRA OPENED DOOR after door along a darkened hallway. Each held the very same man, a guy of about fifty with a shiny bald head. "Have you seen Tess?" she asked each in turn and they all responded negatively in Greek. There was only one door left and she put her hand on the knob. At that moment the earth shook and she tumbled out of her dream and into an SUV.

Pike Hastings looked at her. "Sorry. I tried to rouse you when we hit Falls Bluff, but you were out like a light. I figured nobody could sleep through the cattle guard. It can be a little rough if you're not used to it, though."

She turned to look behind her, but there wasn't much to see. In fact, there wasn't a whole lot to see no matter which way she looked. Just mountains, fences, trees, a long line of power poles straight ahead and an endless stretch of rolling pastures. For a woman used to towering skyscrapers and hordes of people, it was disconcerting to see so much…nothing.

"Is this it?" she said. "Is this your ranch?"

"You sound disappointed."

"I'm sorry," she said quickly. "It all looks very… peaceful."

"It can be," he agreed.

She studied him again. He'd taken off the cowboy hat when he got behind the wheel, so she could see his profile clearly and there was nothing about it anyone could fault. The occasional flash of his dark blue eyes as he addressed her was pretty darn galvanizing as well, as was the clarity of his expression. He did not look like the kind of guy who lied or cheated or bamboozled, and she should know—she'd met her fair share of all of the above.

Of course, that could just mean he was really good at dissembling, but she kind of doubted it. Wearing jeans and a leather jacket, he looked decidedly casual and yet also as though he could fit in almost anywhere. This was a trait she valued as a detective. It was fine to stand out when you needed or wanted to, but you also had to be something of a chameleon to get the job done.

The drive down the more-or-less straight road seemed to stretch on forever. Here and there crossroads led toward the mountains and she caught glimpses of buildings, perhaps houses. "Is this all Hastings land?"

"It is."

"Do you live in one of those buildings they have in old Westerns?"

"What kind of building do you mean?" he asked with a sidelong glance.

"You know, a bunkhouse."

"No, I live in a barn," he said.

"In a barn!" She sounded incredulous and he smiled.

"Yeah, a barn."

"With animals and everything?"

"Yeah," he said, with another quick glance. "This your first ranch?"

"You can tell?"

"I just guessed." He drove up a hill and suddenly the view changed as a small valley spread below them. Bisected by a shimmering gray river, the acreage on the peninsula that the U-shaped bend in the river created looked stark and icy and terribly remote. A big, old, wood house sat in a protected alcove. Surrounded with covered decks, the house appeared well cared for. What looked like work buildings sat off at a distance. Pale winter light glinted off the frosty shore of the river.

"My father's place," Pike said.

"Is this where Tess is?"

"That's right. She's afraid to be alone."

Sierra gestured at the half-dozen vehicles gathered in the back. "All family," Pike said. "And I'll be damned, Frankie must be here. That's his truck. Haven't heard from him in a couple of weeks, which in and of itself isn't unusual. Of course, him being here probably means he's brought some kind of trouble."

"Frankie is one of your brothers?"

"The youngest. Gerard is the oldest, then Chance and me and Frankie."

"It's hard to watch someone you love struggle with life, isn't it?"

Pike didn't answer right away and then finally he allowed himself a sigh. "I guess that's one way to put it. Of course, he wouldn't think of himself like that. He's just a little more…creative…than your usual cowboy. And lord knows he doesn't back down for anyone." He shook his head and added, "I shouldn't be talking about him."

She looked past his long lashes and the intensity

of his gaze, peering deep into him. "I didn't mean to prod," she said after a moment. "Tess is my only relative and I rarely see her. Apparently I'm rusty when it comes to concepts like family loyalty."

"I don't know. You dropped everything and flew here with very little warning," he said. "Sounds to me like you know exactly what loyalty is about."

"This might be my last chance to make it all up to Tess," she said quietly with a quick sweep of her eyes. "Ever since she disappeared, I've been thinking I should have tried harder."

"Well, you're here now," Pike said. "And that's what counts."

As they pulled in beside the other vehicles, the back door opened. Another tall man, who looked enough like Pike to identify him as one of the brothers, waved from the opening and strode across the yard to meet them, joined by three dogs. One looked like the Lab her father had had for years, and the other two looked like border collies. Sierra didn't consider herself to be much of an animal person, though she could enjoy the simple adoration that shone in a dog's eyes. And you had to admire their perpetual good moods.

One of the dogs jumped on her as she got out of the vehicle, planting muddy paws eight inches above her waist, and she winced as her dry cleaner's disapproving face popped into her head.

"Get down," Pike admonished. He produced a clean cloth from one of his pockets and held it in front of her, staring at the mud, obviously flummoxed by how to help her without invading her privacy as the smear was right across her breast area. She took the cloth from him and wiped off as much as she could.

"Sorry," he said.

"No problem." It had been stupid to wear suede. She'd just figured there'd be more concrete and less dirt.

"Silly dog," the approaching man said as he rubbed the mutt's ears with his left hand and offered Tess his right. "You must be Sierra. I'm Gerard. We're real glad to have you here. I know Pike has been worried about your sister."

"I think everyone has," Sierra said. "Where is she?"

"Upstairs, finally getting some sleep," he said.

Pike hit the side of the blue truck. "When did Frankie arrive?"

"Dad said he sailed in about forty-five minutes ago. He's been waiting for you to get back. He wants to talk to everyone at once."

"Just like my sister wants a family confab," Sierra said. "Must be something in the air around here."

"Is everything okay with Frankie?" Pike asked as he opened the tail of the SUV and took out Sierra's suitcase.

"I'm not sure," Gerard said. "Let's go find out."

Chapter Two

They entered the house as the family almost always did, through the mudroom into the huge kitchen that, as usual, smelled of wonderful food. Roast chicken today, Pike thought, the aroma as welcoming as a holiday hug. From there, they walked into the dining room, and then on to the entryway, where the front door was framed by glass panels. Double doors opened from the entry into the den or office, called different things by different family members but well accepted as the spot where most family discussions took place.

Today a fire burned in the rock fireplace in an effort to stave off the cold air pressing against the windows. For Pike, the chatter of those gathered was like any other sound on this ranch—from the running water of the river to the wind in the tree boughs, the thunder of horse hooves against the summer earth or the faraway braying of cattle. They were the sounds of his past and future, his home.

What did Sierra think of all this? Probably found it confusing as hell. He could picture her in a SoHo loft or a Park Avenue condo, but he couldn't quite fit her into this ranch. He knew there were few things more confusing than meeting a roomful of people who knew each other very well and of whom you knew practically nothing. He also got the feeling that Sierra wasn't the shy type and would cope just fine.

But Sierra pulled on his arm. "Whatever Frankie wants to tell you has nothing to do with me," she said. "I want to see Tess."

"I'll take you to her room," Pike said.

"But your brother is waiting."

"He'll make it a while longer. Let's go see if Tess is awake." He took her muddy jacket and laid it across a chair while quietly perusing the trim white blouse with an almost men's-wear starkness that gave way to some kind of sheer material around the hem. The shirt fit Sierra like a glove and revealed she was much curvier than he'd first thought.

He motioned for her to go ahead of him up the broad staircase leading from the foyer. "The room at the end," he said, directing her to the bedroom in which he'd spent his childhood. They found the door ajar, but the room was dark because the shades had been pulled. It was also warm and steamy. The hum of a humidifier in the corner explained that. The congested sound of Tess's breathing drew Sierra to cross to her sister's bed and stand looking over her slumbering body.

Pike watched her for a minute or two until he felt a hand on his arm. He turned to find Gerard's soon-to-be wife, Kinsey, standing beside him. She jerked her head toward the hallway and he held up a finger. A second later, he touched Sierra's shoulder. She looked beyond him to Kinsey and followed them out into the hall.

After a hasty introduction, Kinsey brought them up to speed on Tess. "I imagine you're disappointed to fly all the way here and find your sister asleep. Dad insisted we call the doctor this morning. Of course, the doctor said you can't really treat a head cold except with steam and acetaminophen and stuff like that. By the time I got back upstairs to start the humidifier for Tess, she'd fallen asleep and didn't even open her eyes as I set things up. She really needs this rest. I could hear her pacing in the guest room half the night."

"I'm not disappointed," Sierra insisted. "What guest room are we talking about?"

"The one at our house," Kinsey said. "Pike and Tess came for dinner last night and Tess wanted to lie down. When she dozed off, I told Pike I'd look after her and he should go home. Unfortunately, she didn't stay asleep long."

"I see," Sierra said. "And you live close by?"

"About a half mile up the river."

"Come downstairs with us and hear what Frankie has to say," Pike suggested.

"No, I'd rather stay here in case Tess wakes up. I have some emails to write, anyway."

"I'll get your suitcase," Pike said.

"Thanks."

"She has a very interesting face," Kinsey said as they walked down the hall. "Good bones, great eyes."

He knew her comment referenced the fact that Kinsey had spent most of her life painting portraits. Since moving to the ranch, she'd developed an interest in still life and scenery as well, and the house she shared with Gerard was filled with her work. She was a small woman with light brown hair and an easy, engaging smile. Come June, she'd marry Gerard.

"She's gorgeous," he agreed. "She doesn't look anything like Tess, though, which I expected but still came as a surprise."

"She doesn't act like Tess, either," Kinsey said.

"Well, she's twelve years older and they haven't lived together for even longer than that. Besides, remember, Tess's latest female role model was my mother."

Kinsey rolled her eyes. She hadn't met Mona, but Gerard had obviously filled her in. All four brothers had different mothers. In fact, Grace, his dad's wife of less than a year, was actually number seven, or lucky number seven as the patriarch of the family fondly called her.

"Do you know what Frankie wants?" Pike asked as they started down the stairs.

"No, but I get the feeling your father does."

She continued into the den while Pike dodged out to the kitchen where they'd left Sierra's suitcase. He lifted it easily and ran up the stairs.

He found Sierra sitting on an upholstered chair

in the darkened room, one long leg folded up under her, head resting on her fist. Their hands touched as he gave her the suitcase and she smiled up at him as she murmured her thanks.

He left without uttering a word, but he didn't want to. Instead, he kind of wanted to stand in the doorway and keep watch. He'd spent his entire life around men until the last year or so. He'd always considered himself a man's man, happiest out on cattle drives, sleeping under the stars.

However, even though Tess had brought tension into his life, he also found her company refreshing. And now Sierra was here and he'd known her all of three hours, but there was something about her, too. Something competent and self-assured, qualities he responded to in anyone and that were downright sexy in a beautiful woman. He knew his link to her was flimsy at best and she'd be gone in a day or two, but he could already feel that he would miss her. For a few moments, while walking down the stairs, Pike wondered if anybody kept her warm at night.

Frankie sat on the fireplace hearth, but as soon as Pike finally entered the room, he sprang to his feet. It was obvious he was excited and Pike took a deep breath, hoping it was for some positive reason and not because he was about to go to jail for something.

Like all the Pike men, Frankie was tall, but his build was a little more wiry than the others and his hair was lighter, especially in the summer. Now, in the midst of winter, it had darkened to Pike's color, but he wore it longer. He also tended to dress a little more *GQ* than anyone else, and today wore dark gray slacks and a light gray shirt that mirrored his eyes.

"Dad has an announcement to make," Frankie said, but Harry Hastings shook his head.

"This is your show, boy. You're the driving force behind it all."

Frankie made eye contact with everyone gathered around him. "I wanted to reveal all this after calving season and before summer work piles up on us, but the producers are anxious to do a little preliminary work. Besides, there's never a time where everything gets quiet and boring around here, especially not lately, right?"

He paused to grin and glance at each of them in turn. Pike had to agree it had been a hectic few months.

"What producers? What are you talking about?" Chance asked from his seat beside Lily. Charlie, her five-year-old son, was still at kindergarten, but Chance gripped Lily's hand in his and it appeared he wasn't letting go. Good for him. When your soul mate comes along, what else can you do but grab on to her and hold tight?

Frankie took a deep breath. "As you guys all know, November is the one hundredth anniversary of the incident at the hanging tree."

He was referring to the bank robbery of the ghost town, or what was left of it now, and the subsequent capture and execution of three of the four thieves. They had paid for their crimes with their lives by dangling from the end of ropes strung up to the big oak tree out on the plateau. The fourth robber had disappeared along with the spoils and had never been identified or caught.

"About a year ago, I met this guy in Pocatello," Frankie continued. "I mentioned the ghost town on our land and the robbery. He'd actually read a diary written by someone who used to live in Falls Ridge, as the town was called back then. He confessed he'd had a life-long fascination with the events that had the killed the town almost overnight.

"Anyway, it turns out he makes documentaries and he wants to do one about Falls Ridge and the bank robbery and the tree and all that. He says there's been some discussion about the mystery guy who got away, so they'd cover that aspect, as well. Originally, they were going to come on out and start filming in late April, but their backers want winter shots and interviews with all of us so the release can be timed to coincide with the anniversary of the events."

His announcement was met with studied silence. "Dad?" Gerard said at last. "This sounds like a good idea to you?"

Pike watched as his father stood up and walked over to Frankie. It crossed Pike's mind that his father probably couldn't have cared less about hosting a bunch of television people and raking up the past. It probably didn't seem like a good idea at all to him, but on the other hand, when was the last time anyone saw Frankie get interested in anything but making trouble? Consorting with legitimate filmmakers was a far cry from his usual scenarios. Assuming they were legit, of course.

"I don't think it will have much impact on most of us," his dad now said. "I researched the company—it's won a couple of awards and is respected within the industry. They showed us a tape of a show they did on a nesting pair of bald eagles—looked like high-quality work and they're bonded and have the right licenses. They've got network backing… Anyway, unless someone can point out some reason to walk away from this that I haven't seen, I say we get Frankie to give them a call."

"I agree," Pike said, throwing in his hat. Not for a minute did he think having movie types around wouldn't get in the way of ranch life and schedules, but so what? "Let's shake things up a little," he added when he glanced at Chance and Lily. After what they'd gone through back in October, he knew the last thing in the world they would want is any kind of stress, but Chance rallied and threw in his agreement.

Lily, however, had a question. "Did you tell them part of the ghost town burned down last year?"

"Yeah," Frankie said. "It's not a problem. Before the real filming takes place, I'll take some machinery up there and move stuff around. Frankly, what happened there adds to the drama of the place."

At this Gerard stood up. "What do you mean 'what happened there'?"

"Not about your wife and daughter, Gerard. That will get mentioned because it's part of the history of the place now, but no one wants to dwell on a personal tragedy like that."

"And what about what happened to Lily up there, and Kinsey?" Chance asked.

Lily shifted in her seat. "Jeremy died there, Frankie, and Jeremy was Charlie's father. Do we have to muck up all that again?"

"Listen," Frankie said as things began to slide south. The ambience of a moment ago had begun to sour. "What happened here in the last year is part of this family's story, but it's not part of the bank robbery. Our experiences have to be acknowledged but they don't have to be the focus. No one wants that."

Harry Hastings clapped Frankie on the shoulder as he looked at each person in turn. "The production people will be here in a couple of days. They want to scope things out. How about we go that far and if issues arise, we reassess things. I personally think Frankie is right. This show will not be about our recent tragedies."

They all agreed that sounded reasonable. Everyone obviously liked the idea of an escape hatch, a back door, so to speak.

"Gary Dodge, he's the documentary guy I told you about, is interested in Kinsey doing some artist renditions of how the town looked and how an angry posse might have appeared."

"I've done a little commercial work," Kinsey said. "This sounds exciting to me."

"And Dad has agreed the crew can stay in this house with him and Grace."

"We have room at our house, too," Kinsey said as Gerard put an arm around her. They looked at each other and exchanged silly grins, then Kinsey spoke again. "Since everyone is here, it might be a good time to tell you that we're getting married a lot sooner than we originally planned."

"But I thought you wanted a late spring wedding," Frankie said.

"We did. But since our baby is due in June—"

She didn't get any further than that. It seemed to Pike that everyone in the room started speaking at once. Half of them were on their feet, slapping Gerard on the back or hugging Kinsey.

Pike took a vacant chair. The house vibrated with the winds of change, from the two women upstairs to all the news and excitement downstairs. He didn't usually dislike change, but he had to admit that today there was a chill inside him that he couldn't explain. He thought of the way Sierra had turned at the airport to look behind them as they drove away and the chill deepened. As if paralleling her unease, he turned now to face the door and found Sierra standing in the opening. She gestured at him and he immediately went to join her.

"Finished emailing?" he asked.

"Finished before I started. My phone doesn't work, just as you predicted, and I don't know the password for your Wi-Fi."

"The password is *ridgeranch*, all lower case, one word," he said. "I know, it's not terribly original. How long have you been standing there?"

"Most of the time," she said. "I didn't want to bother you."

"So, you heard Frankie's plan?"

"I did. It sounds pretty exciting."

He narrowed his eyes as he gazed down at her face. She was only half a head shorter than he; a tall, shapely woman who he suddenly realized had not come down here out of curiosity or boredom. "What's wrong?" he said quickly.

"Tess's breathing is really loud. I'm worried about her."

"Head colds aren't any fun," he said.

"I tried to wake her and she was limp and didn't even open her eyes. Kinsey said she hadn't given her any medications, right?"

"Beyond acetaminophen, no."

"She spent the night at their house," Sierra said, a new element of fear in her voice.

"Yes, but—"

Kinsey walked into the foyer followed, closely by Grace. Though a generation apart, both women were small of stature, dainty and pretty in their own way, which made sense because they were related. In a twist of fate, mother and daughter had been re-united. Sierra towered over them. "Is Tess all right?" Kinsey asked.

"I don't know," Sierra said. "She seems so out of it. Did you talk to her this morning?"

"Of course. Like I said, she had a restless night. I drove her over here late this morning because Pike had left early to get to the airport. She didn't have a lot to say, but she was awake and coherent."

"What are you thinking?" Grace asked.

"I don't know for sure," Sierra said. "She was alone while you were on the phone, right?"

"Yes. By the time I found the humidifier and got upstairs, it had been about thirty minutes," Kinsey said. "She was sound asleep and then you guys arrived."

"If she took something it must have been within that thirty-minute window. But where would she find something to take?"

"I'm pretty sure she didn't bring anything with her from LA," Pike volunteered. "She was traveling light and didn't have any money. She didn't even have the car Doug gave her. God knows how she got here. She wasn't saying."

"Who would know if she found something at this house?"

"I would," Grace said.

"We'd appreciate it if you could look," Pike said.

"Of course I'll look. We'll all look. Come on."

They hurried up the stairs. "We'll start with the bathrooms," Grace said. As the three women started their search of drawers and cabinets, Pike went into his old bedroom and opened the drapes. He sat down beside Tess and picked up her limp hand.

He'd had a college roommate years before who partied himself into a stupor every single weekend, and that was the last time Pike had seen someone so oblivious. He shook Tess's fragile shoulders and called her name. Her eyes opened briefly, she sort of smiled and faded back away. He searched the garbage can and the night table for some indication of what she might have taken.

And then he picked up the phone and called the doctor. By the time Sierra, Kinsey and Grace arrived with ashen faces and a brown prescription bottle, he had already lifted Tess into his arms and was exiting the room.

"An ambulance is on its way," he told them. "I'm going to meet it on the road to cut down travel time. What did you find?"

"Some of your father's sedatives are missing," Grace said with a concerned face. "I don't think very many, but I don't know for sure."

"We're not taking any chances," Pike said. "She's going to get her stomach pumped."

"I'm coming with you," Tess said. He nodded once and they all descended the stairs in a hurry, Tess stopping to accept the blanket and pillow Kinsey pushed into her arms. A moment later, in Kinsey's car now since Pike's still had a saddle in the back, they tore up the hill and down the long, long roadway, Tess prone in the backseat, her head on Sierra's lap, the blanket tucked around her still body.

THEY MET THE ambulance in a pull-off. The EMTs were at the door with a gurney within seconds, hooking up Tess to bags and drips, calling her name. Sierra stood off to the side with Pike, both of them trying to stay out of the way. Pike handed over the prescription bottle and soon after the ambulance took off with sirens wailing while Pike and Sierra climbed back in Kinsey's car and followed behind.

"Where are they taking her?" Sierra asked.

"The urgent care center in Falls Bluff. The doctor will meet us there."

"Why would she do this?" Sierra asked as tears burned her eyes. She didn't know if they were tears of anger or hurt. "She asked me to come, so why would she choose now to drug herself? Is it to punish me?"

"Don't borrow trouble," Pike said, sparing a hand to cover her arm. In the rush to leave the house, she'd forgotten to put her jacket back on and now, with the warmth of his touch, she realized how cold she'd become. "Tess did know you were coming, true, but she also knew it would take most of three hours to get to the ranch from the airport. Kinsey said she heard Tess pacing all night. Maybe she just wanted to get some sleep. If her motives were any more than that, wouldn't she have emptied the bottle?"

Sierra stared at him for a few heartbeats. "I guess so," she admitted. She rubbed her forehead with her fingers. It was difficult to believe that it had been less than twenty-four hours before when she followed Natalia Bonaparte out of New York to that bar and waited for her companion to show up.

A sudden thought popped into Sierra's head, a flash of intuition, perhaps. Was it possible the man last night had been Spiro Papadakis, after all? What if he'd recognized Sierra that first time she walked past their table? Hadn't she detected a glimmer of recognition on his face when their gazes met? Perhaps he'd been spying on his wife spying on him! He could have seen Sierra and his wife meet somewhere. Could it be that he'd learned to hide his accent and sound like he was fresh from the Atlantic City boardwalk at least for a second or two? Had he, in fact, fooled her?

As a non sequitur went, this one was a doozy, but it often happened that way: get your mind flooded with one problem and an insight into another problem floats in to announce itself.

Her laptop was in her carry-on. As soon as they got back to the ranch, she could download the photos onto the computer and then email the images to Savannah. All she'd told Savannah last night was that she wasn't sure if it was Spiro or not and to be prepared for photographs. She'd also asked about accents but hadn't gotten a response yet.

"You've gotten kind of quiet over there," Pike said as they finally left the riverside road and drew close to a small town proclaiming itself Falls Bluff. Icy rain slithered down the windshield as Pike drove to the urgent care center. The town hardly looked big enough to support such a thing, but that's probably the exact kind of community that needed an emergency facility the most.

"I was thinking," she said. "Not just about Tess, but about a case."

"Does that case have anything to do with why

you looked over your shoulder this morning at the airport?" he asked.

She turned to face him as he pulled into a parking spot. "I'm not sure if it does or not," she said, then opened her door. She couldn't believe how her knees wobbled when she stood or the way her heart suddenly raced.

What if she lost her little sister before ever really finding her, or ever really helping her? The thought was intolerable.

Pike shrugged off his jacket and slipped it over her shoulders as she stepped onto the sidewalk. His arm around her suggested he saw or sensed this sudden bolt of numbing fear, and she welcomed his support as they hurried inside.

Chapter Three

Pike leaned against a wall, hands clasping his hat against his chest, legs crossed at the ankles, waiting for Sierra to arrange medical coverage for her sister. No one knew if Tess had insurance, so Sierra had said she would pay the bill with a credit card. Of course, they could call Tess's father and ask him, but Sierra was reluctant to do that until after they spoke to Tess, and right now that was impossible.

Eventually, Sierra joined him in the waiting room and they sat down beside each other. Pike leafed through a magazine. Sierra just stared toward the door leading to the treatment rooms.

After what seemed like an eternity, Dr. Stewart showed up and greeted Pike like the longtime family friend he was, then sat down. Pike introduced Sierra and explained the relationships. There were so many confusing this-person-married-that-person and divorced-a-year-later explanations that some men might have been baffled, but Mason Stewart was one of Henry Hastings's oldest friends and he knew all about Harry's seven wives.

"She's doing well," he said. "After we got everything out of her stomach, we administered activated charcoal and a cathartic to cleanse the rest of her system."

"Is she conscious?" Sierra asked with a tremble in her voice.

"Yes. Talking is tricky for a while because we numbed her throat, but I expect her to recover as expected. Give her a few minutes and you can speak to her. I have to warn you, she seems very agitated."

"She's been that way for the past day or two, ever since she got here," Pike said.

"Do you know why?"

"Not yet. That's why Sierra came to Idaho. We need to talk to her. Something has her spooked."

"Doctor, I have to ask this," Sierra said softly. "Is there any indication that Tess purposely overdosed?"

"She knew you were coming, right?" he asked.

"Yes. My arrival was imminent."

"Let me just say this. Blood tests and stomach contents show she didn't take a whole lot of the sedative, but she hasn't eaten much of anything, it seems, for quite a while, and she is a slightly built girl. Two of those pills will knock Harry out for twelve hours, let alone a kid weighing less than half his weight. If you're worried about suicide, you should get someone to talk to her, but she insists it's just a case of being desperate to get some sleep, and I'm tending to believe her. I'd like to keep her for a few hours but we're not equipped or staffed to have her all night. I don't know if you're aware of this, but Grace actually worked here as a nurse a few years back."

"Pike's stepmother?" Sierra asked.

"Yes. I feel good sending her home knowing Grace can help look after her. I'm going to call her and bring her up to speed. Give the kid a couple of days to recover from all this, okay? Keep things as mellow as you can."

"Absolutely," Pike said and wondered how on earth they would accomplish that feat.

Dr. Stewart stood and they rose, too. "She wants to see you both. Normally I'd suggest she rest, but I don't think she'll be able to relax until she shares whatever has her upset, so you might as well get it over with. We'll let you know when she's ready."

Once again they sat. If Pike had known Sierra longer, he would have tried to comfort her. It seemed almost natural that he should take her hand or put an arm around her. Instead, he decided to distract her with a question. "Tell me about your last case."

"What?" she said as though she'd been thinking of way different things than work. "My case?"

"The one you had to leave to come here."

She shrugged. "I have a client who is separated from her husband. She wants a divorce. She's the one with the money. She signed a prenup that gives him a good hunk of cash if the marriage dissolves unless she can prove he cheated on her."

"And you were employed to gather evidence."

"Yes. So, she got wind he was seeing a woman out of town. I followed that woman to Jersey to a seedy bar. When a man who looked like my client's husband joined the woman, I snapped pictures, but then I decided he was the wrong guy. Now I'm wondering if I made too quick a judgment."

"Why?"

"Gut feeling, I guess."

"Is that why you seem worried about it?"

"I suppose. It's weird, really. There's no reason to second-guess myself, I just do sometimes, and when that happens it invariably proves I noticed something, you know, like subliminally."

"Did you contact your client already?"

"Emailed her, yes. She doesn't like to talk on the phone. She always emails me unless we meet face-to-face, which only happened once. I'll have to look at the pictures again when we get back to your place."

He looked into her green eyes, eyes as clear as ocean-washed bottle glass. What he saw were things he admired in a human being: passion about their life and convictions, truthfulness and the desire to help. "Do you like your job, Sierra?" he asked.

"Most of the time. How about you?"

He smiled. "Most of the time."

The nurse announced they could go see Tess. Sierra didn't need any more encouragement. She walked briskly down the hall, still wearing Pike's jacket, which, while way too big for her, looked sexy as hell on her lithe body. Her legs in the jeans and boots were shapely, tantalizing, and just to prove how long this day was getting, he found himself wishing the two of them were on an island somewhere, on a beach, lots of bare skin and warm sunshine…

"She's in here," a nurse said and the fantasy died a timely death.

Tess was an elfin-like girl with huge violet eyes and sun-streaked short blond hair. She could be very friendly and sweet or she could be testy and secretive, but the last two days were the only time Pike had seen her scared and he hated it.

Sierra immediately leaned over Tess and hugged her, then smoothed her hair away from her face. Tess looked pale and wasted and about ten years old instead of eighteen. Pike took her hand and squeezed it.

"I'm sorry I messed up," Tess said. Her voice was even more hoarse than it had been and her nose was red.

"Don't worry about it," Sierra and Pike said in unison.

"I take Dad's pills sometimes, but they must be different."

Pike bit back recrimination. They could talk about being stupid on another day.

Sierra lowered her voice. "Tess, sweetheart, what's going on?" she asked gently. "What's the matter?"

Pike scooted a chair close so she could sit down. He stood on the other side of the bed.

Tess's eyes filled with tears and she shook her head.

"Start with where you went when you left your dad and Mona's place," Pike suggested.

"Danny," she said.

"Danny? You mean you ran off with that guy you met last summer?" Sierra asked.

Tess nodded.

There was a look on Sierra's face and a tone to the way she'd said "Danny" that rang a few alarm bells in Pike's head. "Who's Danny?" he asked.

More tears rolled down Tess's wan cheeks and she sobbed into her hands. Sierra offered the tissue box and met Pike's gaze, but she didn't say anything. They waited until Tess calmed down. By now she was sitting up as she was apparently unable to handle the tears and congestion in a prone condition. Her breathing was raspy.

"My—my boyfriend."

"They met at the beach," Sierra explained. "He's a lot older than she is and—"

"He's dead," Tess mumbled.

Sierra sucked in her breath. Pike leaned forward. "How did he die?"

"Someone—someone shot him." She buried her face in her hands and cried so hard her whole body shook. Pike hadn't expended much energy in his life being unsure of himself, but he had to admit that in the face of all this grief he wasn't certain where to start.

"Who shot him?" he asked at last.

Tess shook her head.

"Drug dealers?" Sierra asked. "Tess, was he dealing again?"

"I didn't know he was doing that anymore," Tess

mumbled. "After I found out, he promised he'd quit because it scared me. And then we were in the car that Dad bought me, you know, the blue one? We were going to go for a hamburger. He said he had to talk to a friend and he parked outside a yellow house. He took the keys and left me in the car. I waited and waited but he didn't come back out, so I went up to the porch. I heard someone yell from inside and then the door opened and Danny was standing there. He looked straight into my eyes. And then…and then I heard a shot and Danny just collapsed like someone let all the air out of him. I knew he was dead before he hit the floor. A man was standing behind him with a gun in his hand. I—I ran away. I didn't have the car keys, so I just ran and ran."

The last part had come out all in one breath while her voice got more and more ragged until, at the end, they almost had to guess what she was saying. After a few seconds of stunned silence, she added, "The man who killed Danny looked right at me."

"Who was he?"

She shook her head. "I don't know."

"What did the police say?" Sierra asked. "Why didn't someone call Pike or me?"

"I didn't go to the police."

"Oh, Tess."

"All I wanted to do was blow LA. I didn't know where else to go so I came here. But what if he finds me? He has the car so he knows my name, he could find out about me, he could come here and kill… and kill me."

"We have to call the Los Angeles police and your father—"

"No, please, no," Tess begged.

She was shaking so hard by now and crying so pitifully that the nurse showed up at the curtain. "Is everything okay in here?" she asked.

"Maybe some water and another box of tissues," Sierra said, putting an arm around Tess. The nurse hurried away and once again Pike and Sierra exchanged bewildered looks. He could imagine what she was thinking because he was thinking it, too. Tess was in trouble and it was up to the two of them to make it go away.

"You'll be safe at the ranch," he assured Tess as she sipped the glass of water the nurse delivered. "We've had our share of trouble and we know how to take care of ourselves and our own. You'll be safe. One of us will be near you all the time."

This seemed to calm her, and eventually she drifted into an uneasy sleep.

"May I speak with you outside the room?" Sierra whispered to him. They walked down the hall a few paces, then stopped. Sierra looked exhausted and he felt for her.

"I understand where you're coming from," she said in a very soft voice. "I want to make it all go away for her, too. But we can't hide an eyewitness to a murder. She's going to have to grow up real fast starting very soon, because she's right about the murderer knowing who she is. Who's to say he won't come gunning for her next? And you and I have both lived enough to know that safety is an illusion."

"She needed something to hold on to," Pike said. "It was all I could think to offer." He ran a hand through his hair. "But I know what you mean. You're right."

"We need to inform Doug, too. Tess is going to need her dad's support in the months to come. I get the feeling Doug is a path-of-least-resistance type of guy."

"He'll listen to me," Pike said, and he knew it was the truth. He'd bent over backward to be decent to the guy, both for Tess's sake and, truth be told, for his mother's.

"And I need to talk to the police and find out what's going on," she added. "Trouble is, I don't know if any of this can be adequately accomplished over the phone."

"What are you suggesting?"

"I'm not sure yet. We'll have a chance to talk to Tess when we drive back to your ranch. We have to make her see she has an obligation to Danny and society and to herself, too."

He nodded and tried to look positive about their chances, but Pike realized he might actually know Tess better than Sierra did. He'd be stunned if she agreed to return to LA without a fight.

"No way," Tess said. A few hours had passed and she sounded more like herself, though obviously close to the end of her rope from the stress of the past several days. Her nose was still red and her eyes watery.

"Be reasonable," Sierra said gently and reiterated

her conviction that they needed to inform Doug and the police in person.

"I won't go," Tess said. "Pike said I'm safe here, and I believe him."

"You have to talk to the police," Sierra said for about the fifth time. "They'll have questions only you can answer."

"I'll tell you everything I know. You talk to them."

"And leave you here alone?"

"I won't be alone, I'll have Pike. And while you're in LA, you can see my dad and tell him what happened. If he cares. He probably doesn't. Oh, and you can go to Mona's house and get my things."

Sierra had to admit she was a little startled by Tess's refusal to budge. She herself lived in a world of cooperation with law enforcement. She could hardly imagine Tess shirking this basic responsibility. On the other hand, Sierra had seen a man shot dead once, too, and it had shaken her down to her bone marrow. She tried again. "Your dad won't listen to a word I say so there's no point in my talking to him. And Mona is not going to let me rifle through her house looking for your stuff."

"Then Pike should go."

"But if you aren't going to explain things to the police, I have to. Even then, they'll probably have someone in Idaho come debrief you or even send one of their own investigators. And that's a best-case scenario. When they catch the murderer you'll have to testify at his trial. If you don't, they could issue a warrant and make you return."

"I'll do whatever they want as long as I don't have to go back to LA. And if one of you has to talk to Mona and Dad and the other one has to talk to the cops, then both of you go."

By now they were coming over the hill into the main house's yard. The house was well lit, shining like a Christmas-card picture with the clear skies overhead full of twinkling stars. In a way, Sierra hadn't really believed such quaintness still existed.

Grace met them at the back door, fussing and nervous, and for a second, Sierra thought it had to do with them bringing Tess back to this house, but she soon realized she was mistaken.

"It's those television people," she said. "Frankie said they wouldn't come until the weekend but then they got wind a storm is expected and they decided to drive here straight away." She waved an irritated hand and turned her attention to Tess. "Oh, you poor thing. Come with me. We're going to get you all comfy in the downstairs room. I already moved the humidifier close to your bed. I'm going to spend the night with you. It'll be like a slumber party! But don't you worry, Frankie and your Uncle Harry will be on alert. Pike called and gave us a heads-up. You're safe here with us."

"I'll stay with her—" Sierra began, but Tess had already allowed Grace to put an arm around her and lead her down a short hall. Sierra gazed up at Pike, who smiled at her.

"Feel like you've fallen down a rabbit hole?"

"Kind of," she admitted. "I can't believe how stubborn Tess is being."

"She's had quite a day, you know."

She shook her head, a reluctant smile playing with her mouth. "Are you always so kind?"

"Not always, no."

"She's settling in," Grace said a second later when she returned. "She asked if she could stay here with us while you and Pike take a short trip to LA to 'fix things.'"

"I would never ask such a thing of you," Sierra said, horrified.

"Don't be silly. Tess is Pike's sister so she's one of ours. There are more than enough of us to keep an eye on her and I mean that in every sense. You have to remember, she's visited here before, stayed in this house, cared for the horses. She feels at home here in a way, don't you think, Pike?"

"No doubt," he said.

"Exactly. And remember, last summer you took her all around, to see the ghost town and the old gold mine and the hanging tree and the lake up in the mountains? That gives her a sense of place and nothing makes a frightened person more comfortable than a sense of place."

"I wouldn't argue with you," Pike said diplomatically.

"You know what family means to me, Pike. Everything. Go do what you have to do. I'll try getting her used to the idea she's going to have to return to California." She looked closely at Sierra and shook her head. "You look almost as tuckered out as your sister does."

"I'd be happy to sleep in Tess's room," Sierra said.

Grace shook her head sadly. "It's too small for three of us and Dr. Stewart asked that I stay with her through the next couple of nights."

"Then another room?"

Grace was the soul of hospitality and Sierra could see it pained her to have to shake her head. "I'm so sorry. The television people will be here until about midnight and they're taking all our extra rooms. I don't know why they couldn't wait to get here until morning like ordinary people. Pike, I didn't offer your place for lodging, so you have room there for Sierra. Now you get her home and tucked in before she falls over."

Sierra opened her mouth to protest, but what was the point? Grace was doing what the doctor ordered and the truth was she was so tired that her ability to process any more information seemed doubtful.

"I believe Gerard put Sierra's suitcase in your SUV so it's ready to go," Grace added, directing her comment to Pike. "He said to leave Kinsey's car here and he'd pick it up later. And Sierra, I spot-cleaned your jacket. It's hanging in the closet—Pike, get it for her, will you? I don't know what to say about your boots," she added.

"I'll brush them, they'll be fine," Sierra assured her.

"I hope so. Gerard told me what happened. I don't

know what got into that dog. Give me a minute and
I'll put soup in a thermos so Pike won't have to cook."

They left a few minutes later, laden with soup and
freshly baked bread. Sierra had finally given Pike
back his jacket, and hers, while clean as a whistle
and way better fitting, wasn't as comfortable as his
had been.

"What exactly did Grace mean when she said
that thing about family meaning everything?" Sierra asked as they walked to Pike's vehicle.

"Don't most people feel that way?"

"Yes, but there was another quality in her voice."

"Grace is actually Kinsey's mother as well as her
mother-in-law. Kinsey was raised by her grandmother
after her grandmother killed her father."

Sierra stopped walking. "Wait, are you saying
Grace's mother killed Grace's husband?"

"That's what I'm saying. Of course, it didn't go
down so cut and dried. She was eventually exonerated but it tore the family apart for over two decades."

Sierra continued walking, and when they reached
the SUV she sank into the passenger seat with a
sigh. "I'm so tired I could sleep standing up," she
commented, and as the headlights swept the dark
road ahead, she closed her eyes and didn't open them
again until the vehicle slowed down.

Pike pulled up in front of a red barn. Illuminated
pillars stood on either side of a large double door.
As she watched, a plump yellow dog nosed its way
through a dog flap, yawning and stretching and wag-

ging its tail. The dog moved to Pike's side of the car and when he opened the door, he spoke to her.

"Hey, Daisy," he said, and ran his hand along the dog's head. "Did we wake you up?"

"This is the barn you live in?" Sierra asked as she got out of the car, wary lest this dog jump on her, too. But Daisy seemed to only have eyes for Pike and attached herself to his side as he retrieved Sierra's suitcase and unlocked the door.

"Yep. Come inside. It's freezing out here. Those film people are right, we're going to have snow by the weekend."

He switched on lights and she found herself in a huge open space with rafters high above the floor. A wall covered with all sorts of shelves housed books and all sorts of other things, including a small painting of Pike wearing glasses, sitting on a hay bale, his expression inscrutable.

"Kinsey's work," Pike said. "If you sit down for too long, she draws or paints you."

"She's good."

"Yeah. And before you think I'm the kind of guy who goes around framing pictures of himself for display, Kinsey gave me that for Christmas and placed it right where it sits."

"Aw, shucks," she said in a passable Texas accent. "It never crossed my mind you were that kind of guy."

There were a few open doors off the long wall and Sierra saw part of an office through one doorway and the edge of a bed through another. The kitchen was at the south end of the barn, the living area set up in the middle. The second floor was open and accessible by a broad wooden stairway. A wood-burning fireplace was currently unlit while a fuzzy dog bed occupied one cozy corner.

Daisy had retreated to her cushion, her gaze fastened to Pike but darting to Sierra now and again as though keeping track of the competition. "Your dog can't take her eyes off you," Sierra said.

"She's practicing for motherhood, I guess."

"She's going to have puppies?" When Pike nodded, she added, "When?"

"A couple of weeks. The vet said it's her first litter."

"You don't know if she had puppies before?"

"No. I've only had her three months. Found her Halloween night. She'd been hit by a car and was out on the road. Thankfully, she wasn't too badly hurt, but no one claimed her and now she's mine."

"She's a yellow Lab, right?"

"Mostly. There might be something else in there, too, who knows. Have a seat. It's kind of late to start a fire in the fireplace but I'll turn up the heat and put the soup on the stove."

"Let me help you," she said, knowing that if she sat on the comfortable-looking sofa she probably wouldn't get up until morning.

"Sure."

In the end, she sat at the counter and drank a glass of wine he poured her while he heated minestrone soup and toasted slices of bread. She liked watching him move around the kitchen. She'd noticed how fit and handsome he was the minute she saw him—it was just impossible to miss. And now, when the hard day had honed some of his edges while softening others, she admitted to herself he was a very hot guy.

"Are you dating anyone?" she asked.

He spooned steaming soup into a bowl and set it in front of her. "Not currently. Why? Would you like to sign up?"

"I'm kind of over long-distance dating," she said.

"I take it you aren't…involved with anyone?"

"Nope. My last boyfriend moved to France when his company transferred him. We tried to keep it together, but it didn't work. How about you? Any cowgirl's heart go pitter-patter when she sees you?"

"Well, there's a kid about Tess's age at the feed store who has had a crush on me for about five years."

"Do you like her?"

"Patty? She's a nice girl, but she's a kid. I like women."

"Tall women?" she asked, then took a sip of the soup while keeping her gaze on him. Grace was a good cook.

"Yeah," he said as he sat across from her with a bowl of his own. He pushed the basket of bread her way and added, "I'm partial to redheads with green eyes."

"That describes me," she said with feigned surprise.

He looked at her as though just noticing her appearance. If she hadn't seen him checking her out a half-dozen times that day, she might have fallen for it. Another grin and he laughed.

"Well," Sierra said, "besides the distance issue, we have another problem. How are we going to handle Tess?" The spoon was halfway to her lips when a large black shape landed on the counter near her elbow. She threw up her hands and the spoon went flying.

"Sinbad, get down," Pike demanded and Sierra finally realized the shape belonged to a svelte black cat with yellow eyes. The cat meowed and jumped to the floor, where it proceeded to walk away as though offended.

"How many animals do you have?" she asked.

"Just these two, who hang around inside the barn. Of course, there are a lot of others outside. This is a ranch, remember?" His gaze dropped to her bosom. "And you have soup all over your blouse.

Sierra looked down at her shirt and winced. The dry cleaner's image appeared again.

Pike replaced her spoon with a fresh one and they finished the soup with idle chatter until Pike sighed. "Looks like you and I are going to LA."

She nodded. The thought of more travel wasn't exactly comforting right at that moment.

"Let's get it over with, okay? I can arrange plane tickets for tomorrow."

"Okay. Make the flight late enough that I can talk to Tess in the morning and get details about everything she saw and heard."

"Yeah. I have some ranch work I need to finish

up, as well. I'll see if I can get an evening flight. You have to feel like a dead man walking. Let me show you to your room."

Sierra nodded. The promise of lying down was the only thing still keeping her on her feet. He toted her suitcase for her, depositing it on top of a dresser in a small room bright with white paint and pine walls. "There's a bathroom behind that door in the corner. This house is wireless. I know you had business you wanted to take care of. The password is *PIKESPLACE*, one word, all caps."

"You seriously need to work on creating secure passwords," she said with a smile. "However, work can wait until tomorrow, too," she said, but kind of knew she'd get started on it before she fell asleep.

"This can't wait," Pike said and stepped close to her. Staring down into her eyes, he touched her cheek, tilted her chin up, leaned down and kissed her. His lips were vibrant and fabulous and the kiss way more impactful than she would have guessed. It took all her willpower not to pull him back when he moved a few inches away.

"Been wanting to do that since the first moment I saw you," he said, his voice as warm as a caress.

"Me, too," she admitted.

He kissed her briefly again. "Good night, Sierra. Sleep well."

Sierra stripped down to her underwear and hurried under the blankets. The barn was chilly. She'd retrieved her laptop, turned it on and waited for it to boot. The bed was soft and comfortable and the pillow felt like a little cloud. The memory of Pike's tender and unexpected kiss spread contented tendrils throughout her body. Consciousness lasted about ten more seconds before she fell asleep in the glow of the computer screen.

Chapter Four

Sierra woke up early to find the black cat staring at her from his perch on the nightstand. She sucked in a surprised gasp of cold air that startled the creature. He jumped to the floor and disappeared out the door and she showered and dressed quickly.

She felt rested but a little at odds. She'd been dreaming, she realized, and though she couldn't recall the content, she did know it hadn't been pleasant.

Her first thought was of Tess and she picked up her phone and opened her bedroom door. Then she saw the time and decided not to call yet. Instead she wandered over to the painting she'd seen the night before, the one of Pike wearing his glasses.

Kinsey had caught the intelligent glint in his eyes and the angular shape of his face. Sierra had seen each of the brothers and they were all handsome, virile men, but they were all different, too. In the past, she might have been attracted to Chance or Frankie, who each exuded a hint of wild spirit close to the surface. Pike was not usually the kind of man toward whom she gravitated. He was a serious guy with a quiet, strong core; too intense for her, or so she might once have thought. But now he occupied all the spare nooks in her mind.

She used her phone to take a picture of the painting, and then she shot another of a framed map of the Hastings ranch. The place was huge, but at last she saw where the houses were in relation to one another, where the so-called hanging tree ruled a portion of a plateau and the location of the ghost town. She was turning away when a small bronze statue of a man standing beside a horse caught her attention and she snapped a photo of that, too.

A clicking sound announced the arrival of Pike's dog, Daisy, who seemed to be smiling as she wagged her tail. "You look like you're going to pop pretty soon," Sierra told the dog. Was that the first animal she'd ever addressed as though she could understand the words? Maybe.

Eventually, she started a pot of coffee and settled down on the sofa to read emails and to study the photos she'd taken at the bar.

"OUR PLANE LEAVES at six o'clock tonight," Pike announced when he found Sierra sitting on the couch fooling with her laptop. "Do I smell coffee?"

"I put on a pot, hope you don't mind," she said. "Come look at something."

He joined her on the sofa. Whatever soap she'd lathered with hadn't been found in his shower, he was sure of that. Nothing he owned smelled quite like flowers mixed with sunshine. A pair of eyeglasses sat on the table in front of her. "I didn't know you wore those," Pike said.

"They're clear glass. There's a camera in the bridge piece."

He smiled. "Very James Bond."

"They work pretty good. My dad's old cohort taught me to use them when I was a kid."

"Was he a private eye?"

"Nope, he was Dad's campaign advisor, Rolland Bean. Everyone called him Rollo."

"Was your dad in politics?"

"He was on the city council. Then he ran for mayor of Dusty Lake, New Jersey, and lost in a landslide. Rollo and his creepy son, Anthony, kind of disappeared after that."

He smiled at her and leaned in closer. There was a smile twitching her lips as she spoke and he wasn't sure if it was because of old memories or the fact they were mere inches apart. "Why do you say his son was creepy? Creepy in what way?"

"Hmm. Well, his eyes were two different colors. One brown, one gray, which was kind of cool, but he was always lurking around, buttering up the adults, you know, then acting superior to the kids. And he was sneaky mean." She fussed with the machine and brought up two photos on the screen. "Tell me what you see."

"A man in two different places," he said. One photo showed a guy standing at a counter, looking back over his shoulder. The other one showed the same guy sitting in low light. "Who is he?"

"The one ordering coffee is Spiro Papadakis. He's the husband of the wealthy client I told you about."

"The one who wants to protect her money in a divorce," he said.

"That's right. A day or two before, Savannah—she's my client—hired me. Her girlfriend swore she saw Spiro at a New Jersey bar with the woman in this picture. It so happened the girlfriend knew the woman he was with because they'd worked together at a junior college a few years back. Savannah didn't want me to follow Spiro because she was afraid he'd make my tail and use that against her, so I opted to follow the woman. The first night she went to a retro disco place in New York City, met a guy there and flirted like crazy. I finally left when they did. She went to his place and since he was twenty years too young to be Spiro, I went home. They were so hot and heavy with each other that I thought for sure the girlfriend had been mistaken, maybe not about Spiro but about Natalia. Anyway, the next night Natalia drove out to Dusty Lake, New Jersey, and went into Tony's Tavern, which is the same place the girlfriend saw her at a few days before. Natalia waited there for the man who looked like Spiro to show up. It seemed I had everything I needed until I heard the guy speak. Spiro is Greek and by all accounts has a pretty distinct accent. The guy in the bar sounded like a longshoreman. I thought I struck out."

Pike put on his glasses and studied the photo. "There's damn little to identify either one of them. No scars, no distinctive anything."

"Just their watches," Sierra said. "His is hard to see, but hers looks like diamonds."

"Real diamonds?"

"Who knows? As a counselor she can't make that much money, but she lives in a nice place and her clothes are fabulous. She doesn't strike me as a girl who wears fakes."

"What does Savannah say about the pictures?"

"I don't know yet. I just emailed a whole slew to her." She opened her email and clicked. "I copied the email to myself. This is what I sent."

He whistled. "That's a lot of photographs."

"If nothing else, I'm thorough," she said with a chuckle. "Now listen to this. Savannah responded to the accent thing and that's what makes it interesting. She said Spiro was an actor back in Greece and still dabbles in small productions. According to her, he can adjust his voice. So now I'm back at square one."

"This is fun, isn't it?" he said.

"You mean like putting together a puzzle?"

"Yeah."

She smiled at him. "It can be." She closed the laptop and studied him for a moment. "You look pretty damn sexy in those glasses."

He picked up the tortoise frames and settled them on her face. It was hard to imagine a look she couldn't pull off. "You're kind of cute yourself," he said, and they exchanged bemused smiles. He wasn't sure why he felt so comfortable with her. By all rights, she should make him uneasy. They were two worlds colliding and yet there appeared to be a little pool of commonality between them.

"I'm going to rustle up some breakfast and then we'd better head over to the house and get things moving," he said.

She grinned at him. "I don't believe I've ever seen anyone rustle before. Mind if I watch?"

THIS TIME THE unexpected vehicle parked beside the main house was a bright blue van with the initials LOGO on a plaque attached to the door. It bore a Washington State license plate.

"Looks as though the television people arrived," Sierra said.

They went inside to find three men standing around the granite counter sipping from mugs of coffee. Pike's dad was facing them, hands on his waist, frown on his long, lean face. Tension was thick in the air.

Tess, nose dripping but looking better than the day before, sat nearby on a stool. She wore the same fuchsia T-shirt she'd worn the day before, though it appeared to have been freshly laundered, and pink loafers. It occurred to Sierra that the girl had run away without a change of clothes.

Introductions were made, all too fast to remember for more than a few seconds. The man in charge looked about fifty, with gray on his temples and wire-framed glasses. He introduced himself as Gary Dodge.

"Is something wrong?" Pike asked.

Gary said, "Not really," at the same time Pike's dad said, "Hell, yes. They've got legal troubles!"

"Now, that's an overstatement," Gary said in a calm, reassuring voice. He spread his hands on the counter and addressed Pike, obviously anxious for a different perspective. "We have one former disgruntled employee who tried to sue us for wrongful termination. He lost, but since then weird things have been happening and we're about one-hundred-percent positive he's behind it all. He's made things…difficult…for us lately, with nuisance calls and sporadic crazy behavior, but we don't believe he poses a threat to anyone's safety."

"You told me his behavior was getting more erratic," Harry said.

Gary swallowed and nodded. "Yes, I wanted to be honest with you. Listen, we're all set to go on this project. We've done a year's worth of groundwork and no one wants to walk away. It's true that last August this guy somehow canceled our caterers on a desert shoot and we went thirsty and hungry for a day. And last month he broke into our headquarters and destroyed a couple of computers and ransacked the safe, trying to destroy this project. But we always have backups and nobody has ever been hurt."

"I don't know," Pike said. "It seems to me people like this keep upping the ante. Why haven't the police stepped in?"

Gary's eyes shifted to his hands. "We haven't called them," he said.

"Why not?"

"Because we can't prove anything and we don't want the bad publicity."

Or their insurance and backers to get nervous, Pike thought. He kept that to himself. "So, what's the upshot?" he asked.

"We'd like to go ahead with everything as it's planned. Your father is understandably nervous about the possibility this guy would make trouble for you. I've been trying to explain that, so far, he's only made trouble for us."

"There are women and children living here," Harry said.

Gary cleared his throat. "Listen. We'll only be here a couple of days. What if we hire a protection agency to secure this place?"

"More people?" Grace said from the stove where she was frying sausages. The tone of her voice made it clear what she thought about that idea.

"Just a couple."

"I don't know," Harry said. He turned his gaze to Pike. "What do you think?"

Pike shrugged. "What does Frankie say?"

"He says since when does a Hastings get scared of a lunatic? The boy is anxious for this project, you know that."

"He isn't the kind to back down from a challenge," Pike said and, addressing Gary, added, "Personally, I appreciate your disclosure, but I don't think we need anyone to watch our backs in the winter. There are a lot of us here and we're all experienced with weapons and, lately, with our share of homicidal maniacs. Come the fall when we're up to our ears in ranch business, that's a different story. Let me talk to Frankie. Where is he?"

"He and Oliver went out to your barn," Gary said. Then he jammed his hands in his pockets and added, "I hesitate feeding fuel to the fire but there's one more thing you have to know."

"Now what?" Harry barked.

"In the interest of transparency, the talent we had lined up to do the voice-over had a stroke earlier this week. He's pulled out of the project."

"What does that mean for us?"

"It doesn't mean anything for you right now. It means that we shoot the winter scenes as planned and then I start looking for someone else."

"One issue at a time," Pike said. He smiled at Sierra and Tess and started out to the barn.

Lily arrived home from driving her son to the end of the road to catch his school bus as Pike left the mudroom.

"Things still tense in there?" she asked.

"Kind of."

"Oh, goody."

He patted her fondly on the back and walked to the barn, where he found Frankie talking with a fourth man, who introduced himself as Oliver. This guy was a head shorter and a decade older than Frankie. A bag of camera equipment hung over his shoulder and all three ranch dogs sat by his legs staring up at him.

"Dad still fussing?" Frankie asked.

"Some. What's with the dogs?"

Oliver laughed. "I gave them an old cracker I found in my camera bag. Now they're my new best friends."

"Surest way to their hearts is through their stomachs," Frankie said with a grin.

Pike told Oliver that breakfast was almost ready over in the house, and Oliver loped off, dogs trailing behind him. "Let's ride over to the feed barn and make sure the tractors are ready in case the storm they're predicting comes and we need to haul hay to the cattle," Pike said. "We need to talk about the documentary, anyway."

They saddled their horses and headed out, talking as they rode. Frankie was adamant. "Everything is going to be fine," he said.

"What about the loss of the actor who was going to do the voice-over?"

Frankie shrugged. "Oliver says they'll find someone else. I'm not worried about it."

"Then let's just tell Dad we think the project should continue."

"I agree. He's just being cautious."

"That's in his job description," Pike said.

By the time the day had passed, he had started to sort out the documentary people. From what he gathered this advance team consisted of Oliver, who was the cameraman, Gary the producer, an assistant producer named Ogden and a story consultant named Leo. In other words, Pike figured out at last, LOGO was an acronym for their first names. Did that mean that this crew was pretty much the whole company?

"Just about," Gary said when Pike asked. "We hire freelancers for other positions on a as-needed basis. Like, we have an historian working for us right now and today we engaged your soon-to-be sister-in-law, Kinsey Frost, to produce a series of sketches and paintings to illustrate past incidents." He paused and smiled. "I want to thank you and your brother for convincing your father to give us a chance."

"You might think about hiring an investigator to uncover the truth about your sabotages," Pike said.

"Yeah. I actually talked to Ms. Hyde this afternoon and she gave me the name of a guy who works in Seattle."

Pike arranged for Frankie to stay in his house to keep an eye on Daisy while he was gone, and before too long it was time to drive to Boise. Five hours later, the plane touched down in Los Angeles, and an hour after that, thanks to traffic, they walked into the lobby of the hotel Pike had booked for them. They agreed to meet for dinner in thirty minutes.

As it happened, a half hour later they arrived at the elevator at the same time. "Nice hotel," Sierra commented as they rode down to the lobby.

"I stayed here the last time I came to see Tess."

"Not at your mother's house?"

"No, I take her in small doses."

"Her and Doug both."

"Actually, Doug is better than the husband before him. The only good thing that man ever did was die young."

She laughed. "And leave your mother a big old house and a boatload of money."

"True."

The restaurant downstairs had a free table, so they decided to eat there and both ordered a pasta dish and a glass of wine. "So, what did your client say about the photographs?" he asked her.

"She just emailed me that the guy in the bar was her husband."

"Wow. End of case."

"Well, no, actually, just the beginning. We're going to meet when I get home to figure out the next step. She'll need more intimate photos than the ones I shot if she needs to make her case to a judge."

"Is she hard to deal with?"

"A little. Like I said, she has a phone phobia so we seldom talk, and she's something of a recluse. She was Miss Georgia a couple of decades ago. I think that's how she nabbed Spiro. If I can catch her husband in a really embarrassing situation her lawyer might be able to convince him to sign away his rights to the prenup and she can be done with him even faster."

"Do you do many divorce cases?"

"My share. A lot of what I do is computer work. Background checks and things like that. By the way, I should have mentioned that I called the Los Angeles Police Department this morning and spoke to a Detective Hatch. I told him everything Tess told me and he said he would start looking into it so he'd have some news to share when I go see him tomorrow."

"I thought you didn't think this was a conversation to have over a phone," Pike commented.

"I didn't. But unless we want to be down here for more than a day or two, I decided the police had to be told in advance. Plus, if they're sitting on a homicide while their star witness hides away in Idaho, they're bound to get upset."

"I agree," Pike said. "Did he mention any dead drug dealers?"

"Nope. Said there were only two local unidentified bodies and they were both female, but who knows what he found out today."

The rest of dinner probably appeared relaxed to an onlooker, but there were rivers of tension flowing underneath. Beyond the stress of the coming commitments, there were undercurrents of awareness between the two of them. Pike couldn't help but be hyperaware of Sierra's lips as she spoke, of the way she chewed, the way she leaned forward to hear what he was saying. There was the memory of their very brief kiss and the lack of any kind of restraint between them, to say nothing of lingering eye contact.

So it came as a little bit of a disappointment when she kissed him good-night on his cheek and thanked him for her meal. He pulled on her shoulder as she started to unlock her door and she turned around, her eyes questioning.

"When do we see Detective Hatch?"

"I thought we were going our separate ways," she said. "The police department isn't far from here. I can take a cab while you drive out to Mona's house.

I assume you have to ask her where Doug went after she kicked him out?"

"I do, but I'd rather we stick together. I'm as anxious to hear what the police say as you are. And if we're going to fight for what's right for Tess with her father, we should show a united front."

"That makes sense," she said. "I told Hatch eight o'clock."

"Fine." He ran his fingers along her silky jaw. "That's not really why I detained you, you know that, right?"

Her smile shot through him. "I kind of figured. But I also think we should get some sleep. Let's give ourselves a little time to catch our breath."

"How about a friendly kiss good-night?" he asked.

She smiled. "That couldn't hurt, could it?"

"No, that couldn't hurt," he agreed and touched his lips to hers. He'd intended it to be light and informal, but the fuse that was lit between them changed things. She raised her arms to circle his neck. Her breasts beneath her sweater pressed into his chest. Her lips parted, and her mouth was warm and inviting. He'd never been so intensely aware of a woman as he was of her.

"I could get addicted to you," she whispered when at last they separated.

"That's fine with me," he murmured, his lips against her cheek.

"We live such different lives."

"Is that what's worrying you?"

She nodded as she touched his face. If she wanted

him to slow down, she was going to have to send clearer signals. "I'm not against a casual affair as long as everyone understands that it's terminal," she said softly, her fingers caressing his ear.

"And you don't think I can handle that?"

Her lips touched his again. "I'm not sure. I don't even know if I can. I think I need to say good-night, Pike. I'll see you in the morning."

"Good night," he said and waited until she'd opened the door and retreated inside, sparing him one last smile before the door closed.

DETECTIVE RICHARD HATCH was a guy of about forty with a framed photo of a woman and three young children sitting on his desk. His fair hair was cut in a buzz cut, his skin was tanned a light brown, suggesting he spent time at the beach when off duty, and his crisp white shirt would probably look more in place back east than in the easy breezy climate of Southern California.

Sierra had dressed in her black jeans and newly brushed boots. She wore her leather jacket over a white tank. Pike looked down-home comfy and incredibly good in his usual garb of boots, jeans and a shirt. The clothes might be ordinary, but the man inside them was so well put together that he elevated them.

She decided she was fixating on all these details to keep from being nervous about what she was about to hear Hatch say.

He spread his hands on his desk. "I got nothin'," he said.

"Nothing? What does that mean?" Sierra asked.

"It means no dead body, no evidence of a shooting, no street news."

"What about Danny Cooke?"

He thumbed through a small stack of papers. "Daniel Robert Cooke. Twenty-seven years old, born in Detroit, Michigan. He's been in and out of trouble his whole life. The nature of the crimes escalated as he got older. You know, he shoplifted when he was eight, robbed a bowling alley when he was thirteen, used a weapon in his next robbery. In and out of jail, lots of drug charges. Moved out here about nine months ago. He's been a guest in our jail a few times, all drug related, all in and out. Don't know when he started dealing for sure."

"Did you find anyone he did business with, or who may have known him on a personal level, like as a friend?"

"No. But I spoke to his landlord, a Mr. Fred Landers, who happens to live in the adjoining duplex. He bought in to the community a long time ago and then watched it get overrun with gangs. Anyway, he saw Danny and your sister leave that afternoon. This was after an altercation between them. He didn't hear what was said, just that there was an angry exchange of words and that apparently it wasn't uncommon. He said Danny was shouldering a backpack the landlord had seen your sister carry on occasion. They drove off in a blue car.

"Three hours later, he saw Danny drive into the duplex driveway and get out of the car alone. He walked into the house and the landlord heard the usual noises. Then Danny came back out, threw a few things into the car and took off. The landlord had a weird feeling about things so he went over and found the apartment empty with the key on the table. It wasn't the first time someone had run out on the rental and since he'd been more or less expecting something like that to happen, he wrote if off to the drugs he knew Cooke used."

"Was he positive it was Danny who returned?" Sierra asked.

"He said he was. I don't know. Sometimes people just see what they expect to see. The view from the window he admitted looking out of wasn't great."

"Why had he been expecting something to happen?" Pike asked.

"Danny talked constantly about returning to Detroit. The landlord figured they must have had a big fight and Danny abandoned Tess somewhere, taking the car and moving out before she got back to the apartment. By the way, the landlord thought your sister used drugs, too."

"She doesn't. I checked her arms."

"Maybe weed?"

"Maybe. She says no. Did you check on whether Danny made it back to Detroit?"

"Talked to his mother this morning. She hasn't heard from Danny in a year or more and says she doesn't expect that to change. She's heard no word he's back in town."

He set the papers aside and folded his hands. "We went to the house you told me about, the one where your sister claims Danny Cooke was killed. We found absolutely nothing suspicious. The woman who lives there, Inez Ruiz, is an elderly lady with poor hearing who's resided at that address for twenty years. It took us forever to get her to answer her door. Says she's afraid of what's outside. Forensics gathered samples from the area right inside the house, but without further evidence, this will get low priority. You're familiar with how big-city departments are run, Ms. Hyde. It's not like television. Things take time and when there's so little to go on—no body, no witnesses—"

"Except my sister," Sierra interjected.

He nodded. "Yeah. Except a kid who may or may not use drugs, who was living with a known drug dealer and who waited a week before telling anybody what she saw. Ms. Hyde, I think your sister is the victim here. The victim of a boyfriend who wanted her car and not her. I suspect Danny is alive and well and knows that he scared her enough to keep her quiet."

"Would you mind if I go to the neighborhood and ask a few questions?" Sierra asked. "I understand where you're coming from, but she described Danny's death in such painful detail, I have to give her the benefit of the doubt."

"Knock yourself out, but be warned. This is a high-crime, gang-regulated part of the city. Tread lightly. And I know it's painful, but keep an open mind when it comes to the possibility that your sister was high and either thought she saw things happen that didn't, or is lying because she lost her car to her drug-dealing boyfriend."

"Thanks," Sierra said, her voice tight. She glanced at Pike, who hadn't said a word past the introduction. "Do you have anything you want to ask the detective?" she asked.

He sat forward. "Has anyone found her car?"

"Well, no one has looked for it because it wasn't reported stolen. Your sister or her father, whoever is the legal owner, should file a report."

"Okay," Sierra said.

"One last thing," Pike added. "Are you sure you got the right house?"

"The house where the reported shooting took place?"

"Yes," Pike replied. "Tess seemed relatively vague about exactly where it was."

"I went on the information I was given," the detective said. "Middle of the block, North Ash, red door. I'm pretty sure we got the right place." He stood up and offered his hand to each of them in turn, then slipped Sierra an index card. "These are the addresses and the names of the people I spoke to. I'll keep my eyes open and stay in touch. You do the same."

"Thank you," she said. She and Pike left the department in silence, both lost in thought. Did Tess use drugs? Had she imagined the whole thing or had Danny faked his death to end their relationship? Even more painful was the thought that Tess might have lied to her and Pike.

Sierra wasn't sure what the truth was, but she knew she better find out.

Chapter Five

Through mutual agreement, they decided the morning might be best spent trying to find out where Doug had gone after Pike's mother kicked him out of her house instead of tackling a gang-orientated neighborhood that probably wouldn't come alive until later in the day.

The traffic was grueling and the only thing that made it halfway tolerable was the fact that Sierra sat next to him in the car. She was fooling with her phone and at last she looked up. "It's twenty degrees in New York and twenty-eight degrees in Idaho," she announced. "And it's seventy-eight degrees here."

He smiled as he gazed at the sky. Under a veneer of smog, it was indeed clear and bright. He didn't tell her he'd take cold, crisp air any day to this, but that was the truth. "I think we better plan on leaving by tomorrow night or we stand a chance of getting frozen out of Boise," he said. "I read the anticipated storm is due to hit by Friday night."

At last they pulled into Mona's driveway. The house was circa 1950, a big old mansion of a place surrounded by grounds that kept two gardeners busy three days a week. It was a good thing that Mona's previous husband had left her cash as well as the house.

"This is the first time I've been here," Sierra said. "Tess sent me pictures a few years ago. It's a great old place."

"It is that. I'm surprised you never came to visit your sister, though."

"Well, neither Mona nor Doug exactly rolled out the welcome mat. Like so many families nowadays, like yours, for instance, ours was a little complicated. I had my father and Tess had Doug. My mother was our commonality and when she died, well, things got tricky. If we'd been closer in age, maybe I could have shared my dad with her, but it just didn't work out that way. But oh, brother, I loved visiting Dad every summer. He and Rollo always seemed to have something going on."

"Rollo. He's the man who taught you about the camera glasses," Pike said. "The one with the creepy son."

She smiled. "Yeah."

"Sounds like you still miss him."

She fingered the stone at the base of her throat. "You're right, I do. I should have found other ways to stay close to Tess. Maybe I was too judgmental about some of her iffy friends."

"Like Danny?"

"Exactly. She told me about him once and then never mentioned his name again. That's after I came unglued when she said he did drugs and sometimes sold them."

"Did you try to talk to Doug about him?"

"I tried. He wasn't listening. It was right before Mona kicked him out of her house."

Pike shook his head.

"Yeah, well, beating myself up isn't going to change anything, so I'd rather concentrate on fixing what can still be fixed," Sierra added. "But I do have to ask. How did someone like Mona end up giving birth to someone like you?"

"Mona grew up in a small town close to Falls Bluff," he told her as they wound their way up a heavily land-scaped path to the patio by the side door. "She and Dad had a fling after Chance's mother left. When she got pregnant she came to Dad for money to end it. Her only goal was to become a movie star and that did not include a baby. Dad said if she would stay long enough to give birth to me and hand me over, he would finance her in LA for one entire year. Mona took the deal. They got married and then divorced within two months. I grew up with three brothers and a few step-mothers thrown into the mix."

"But Mona never acted, did she?"

"Not in films. A little stage work at first and then she transitioned from being an actor to being an actor's wife."

"Parents do a number on kids sometimes, don't they?"

"I can't complain. The ranch is great and I have people who love me. Can't ask for much more than that."

"I suspect you're an easy guy to love," Sierra said.

He stared down into her hypnotic green eyes, made all the more brilliant by the plethora of greenery around her. His gaze traveled to her peachy lips and she smiled. "This isn't a good time for hanky-panky," she said with a soft laugh.

"'Hanky-panky'? Where in the world did you dig up that old expression?"

"My dad used to say it about certain political figures."

"One tiny kiss," he said and completed the act before she could protest. The next thing he knew, he heard his name.

"Pike! Is that you?"

He turned to look at the house and found his mother standing at the open door.

Thanks to a rigorous diet and exercise program, to say nothing of yearly appointments with a plastic surgeon, Mona DeVry was not only holding her own at age fifty-one, but in the right light, could also easily pass for someone a decade younger. Fine, blond hair brushed the shoulders of a flowing white caftan as she crossed the cement porch to give him air kisses on either cheek. Pots overflowing with flowers couldn't compete with the floral scent of the perfume wafting around her in a delicate cloud. It might only be eleven in the morning, but as usual, her makeup was flawless.

"You look great," Pike told her.

She immediately touched her cheeks, pleasure glowing in her eyes. "Do I? Oh, good. Why didn't you tell me you were coming? You know Tess isn't here, right?"

"Yes, I know. I need to talk to Doug."

"Douglas Foster is a two-timing rat," she said, but there wasn't much malice in her voice. "Why do you want to talk to him?"

"Tess is in Idaho at the ranch. We need to discuss what's going on with Doug, and Tess would like us to bring back the stuff she left here. Do you know where I can find Doug?"

"Tess moved to Idaho?"

"More or less."

"Why would any woman want to go there?" She turned her attention to Sierra and added, "Oh, are you from Idaho? I'm sorry if I offended you."

"No, I'm not from Idaho," Sierra said.

"This is Tess's sister, Sierra," Pike added. For some reason he'd just figured the two women had seen each other in passing or at least a photograph. The lack of communication between Sierra and Tess's California family was mind-boggling to him.

"Nice to meet you," Sierra said.

"I bet," Mona said, irony dripping from her voice.

"Mom," Pike warned.

"I've asked you not to call me that, Pike," she said. "You're far too old for anyone to believe you're my son. And as for you, Sierra, well, all I know about you I learned from Tess and Doug. To one you're an angel, to the other a demon. I bet you never hear conflicting stories about me."

Pike shook his head but Sierra smiled. "That's true, I don't.

"Do you know where Doug is?" Pike asked again.

"Did I hear someone say my name?" a man called from the doorway. It struck Pike that both Mona and Doug had announced themselves and then proceeded to make an entrance like the patio was a stage.

Tightening the belt of a black silk robe around his waist, he sauntered out onto the patio. Back in the day Douglas Foster had been a force to be reckoned with, an approachable, handsome flirt who was also a competent actor. He'd carried a detective series for most of two seasons before he imploded and ended up in rehab. Most people would still recognize him as the voice of a popular insurance company and from guest spots on other shows. He owned a restaurant in LA, but to Pike it appeared his life seemed geared toward the next big break.

However, the only question on Pike's mind at the moment was what was he doing at this house, seemingly wearing nothing but a robe and slippers? "You two are back together?" Pike asked. "I thought he was a two-timing rat."

Douglas grinned, revealing his trademark dimples. In his fifties now, he still exuded a boyish charm.

Sierra spoke up. "Aren't you going to say hello to me, Doug?"

"Sierra, always a pleasure," he said without really looking at her. "I assume you two are here to see Tess."

"Not exactly," she said.

"Then what do you want? I don't know where she is. She hasn't bothered to call me or answer any texts. Frankly, I kind of gave up on her. In fact, I wondered if she was with one of you."

"Is that why you constantly pestered us about her whereabouts?" Sierra replied. The sarcasm wasn't lost on Doug, who frowned.

Pike interceded. "Tess is on my ranch in Idaho, Doug. We're here to talk to you. We're also here to collect some of Tess's things."

"Take her stuff, I don't care," Mona said. "I'll pack it up for you, or at least the maid will. Last I saw of Tess she was driving away with her druggie boyfriend."

"You never told me that," Doug said, and he did look surprised.

Mona shrugged. "Didn't I? Must have slipped my mind. Well, no matter. That girl has been a problem from the day her hormones kicked in. I, for one, am glad she's gone." She took Doug's hand and sidled up against him. "Now we can concentrate on you and me."

"But if you knew she was with that loser, you should have told me."

"I'm telling you now!" Mona said, sounding bored. "Tess ran off with Danny what's-his-name. He probably talked her into driving to Idaho to sponge off Pike."

"Not exactly," Pike said calmly. "According to Tess, Danny never left LA because someone killed him right in front of her."

"He's dead?"

"We think so."

"Is that a bad thing?" She shook her head. "No, don't bother answering that. You'd better come inside." She sighed dramatically and added, "Doug, be a dear and whip up a pitcher of mimosas."

WHILE PIKE TRIED to reason with Doug and Mona, Sierra read the lineup of new texts from Tess. A couple mentioned items she wanted them to be sure to bring from Mona's house, but most were plaintive cries for information concerning Danny. Sierra was stuck saying the same thing every time: No news yet, I'll let you know when we find out anything.

They left after surveying Tess's room, which was crammed with teenage stuff, enough to fill a moving van. Sierra pointed out what Tess considered essential to Mona's maid, Lindy, who nodded but wrote nothing down.

All in all, it was a relief to be alone again in the rental with Pike. "Did you get the feeling Doug was more upset about his missing car than his daughter?" Sierra asked three hours later as they drove toward the neighborhood where Tess and Danny had rented a duplex.

"Well, he was still making payments on the car," Pike said with irony. "At least he's reporting it stolen. Are we close yet?"

She peered down at the map on her cell. "A couple more miles. Doug obviously agreed with the cops—

no body, no murder. It's easier that way. Turn left up here."

She heard a ding on her phone. Tess again: Anything new?

Nothing, Sierra texted back. Was it possible Tess was making this up, or had been drinking or using something and had imagined everything? That's what she wanted to ask, but not in a text.

"My mother seems to think Tess made up the story about Danny to get attention," Pike said in an uncannily parallel feed-in to her own thoughts.

"Do you?"

"No," he said thoughtfully. "How could she have described the house they went to so clearly the detective found it without trouble if she hadn't been there?"

"Just because she knows about the house doesn't mean she couldn't have gone there another time." Sierra thought for a second and added, "Although, why would Tess visit the house of an elderly deaf woman in the first place?"

"She saw something, I'd bet my life on it. But trying to get attention is the kind of motive Mona understands."

It was the kind of motive almost anyone who has had to fight for recognition understands, Sierra knew this. And sometimes the feelings that prompted such behavior weren't conscious ones. "Go straight now, I think we're almost at the duplex."

"Great neighborhood," Pike said as he slowed down when Sierra pointed out the building. He pulled to the curb and they both looked at the ratty place built ten feet from the sidewalk. The two units were joined in the middle with driveways to either side. The unit on the left had a very old pink Cadillac pulled into the carport. The unit on the right had a battered truck and a stack of flattened cardboard boxes littered on the porch as though someone was in the process of moving in. "Looks like Mr. Landers got himself a new tenant," Pike said.

They got out of the car and approached the owner's unit. The door opened about four inches, held in place with a chain on the inside. An older man with a pointed nose looked out.

"Yeah?"

"Mr. Landers, my name is Sierra Hyde. My sister is Tess Foster. She lived in the adjoining duplex…"

"I know who she is," he said. "Her and that no-good Danny Cooke lived there for almost three months. Argued all the time. The cops been to see me. Told them all I know. Want my opinion, the girl is better off without Cooke."

The door closed abruptly.

"Now what?" Pike asked.

"Now we drive to the house Tess described. The detective said it's 1008 North Ash off South Vermont Avenue. It's east of here."

While Tess's old neighborhood had looked shabby and unloved, their new destination seemed to be taking them deeper into an almost alternate world. Iron grills and heavy bars protected windows and doors on small businesses, dark alleys looked like death traps and hordes of young men hung out in front of pawnshops and tattoo parlors. A young woman walking with a child in footie pajamas looked like the personification of innocence until the woman turned and Sierra saw that years of meth use had rotted half her teeth and emaciated her body.

Graffiti was everywhere, lots of it undecipherable without knowing the prevailing gang slang. The thought that Tess had run down these streets by herself in the dark to escape Danny's murderer made Sierra's heated skin break out in a chilly sweat.

They found North Ash a few moments later and parked across the street from 1008. If you didn't count the inordinate number of broken-down vehicles in driveways, torn drapes hanging in dirty windows and dead, lifeless yards, the place looked more or less ordinary. The house in question was a small square stucco structure painted a light yellow with two windows facing the street. The door opened off the driveway and it was indeed red. There was a newish small white car in the driveway that looked out of place here.

A knock produced another chained door, but this time a middle-aged woman peered through the crack. She didn't look old enough to fit the detective's description of the home owner. Sierra said, "Is Mrs. Ruiz here?"

"She's here but you don't want to talk to her," the woman said.

"Actually, we came to ask her about a night eight days ago."

"What time of night?" the woman asked.

"Nine o'clock, more or less."

The woman undid the chain and opened the door a little wider. She had a pleasant, round face with a worried expression and was wearing a pair of bright yellow plastic gloves. Sierra and Pike introduced themselves.

"My name is Camila Sanchez. Inez Ruiz used to go to my church before she became too scared to leave the house. I clean for her once a week and I check on her every morning. She can't talk to you about the other night."

"Because of her hearing?" Pike asked.

"That's one reason. The hearing aids don't work so good and she can't communicate that well with most people. But more than that, Inez goes to bed at seven thirty every night of her life. She goes into her room and locks the door and doesn't come out again until I help her get up and dressed the next morning. Good thing there's a little half bath off her room. Someone told you a lie if they said they saw her at nine at night. It would never happen."

Sierra took out her cell phone and found a photo of Tess taken last summer. "Do you recognize this girl?"

Camila studied the picture, then shook her head.

"By any chance, did Mrs. Ruiz mention that the police had come to see her yesterday?"

"The police! Why would they come here? Oh, it's Raoul, isn't it?"

"Raoul?"

"Her worthless grandson."

"I'm not sure about Raoul. The police came because of a report that there was a shooting."

"Where?"

"Here," Sierra said. "In this house, right by this door." They all looked down at the linoleum.

"Police swabbed the floor looking for blood residue," Pike said.

Camila's forehead furrowed. "You know, funny thing, I noticed the floor had been cleaned last week."

"What do you mean?"

"These floors don't get all that dirty because Inez doesn't go outside and not many people visit, so I only clean them every few weeks—truth is I hate to mop. But last week it looked like they'd been scrubbed clean. I just figured it was my imagination."

"We need to tell the police this," Sierra said.

Camila shook her head. "I would rather not talk to the police."

"It might turn out you can't avoid it," Sierra said. "But for now, why did your thoughts turn to Inez's grandson when we mentioned the police?"

"That one," she said with distaste, "is in and out of trouble all the time. He's a loose cannon."

"Does he visit Inez?"

"No. Not since I changed the locks when I found out he was using her house to crash. Him and his drug friends. Poor Inez didn't even know he was doing this. I was just glad she'd started locking herself in her room. I don't trust that boy."

"Let me get this straight," Pike said. "Raoul would

wait until his grandmother had locked herself in for the night and then sneak into the house and spend the night here?"

"Him and his friends. Eat her out of house and home. Most of the time I guess they just slept it off. but sometimes they partied. I know because I picked up the garbage. I wanted to turn him in, but Inez would have hated that…and, well, ever since my own kid had a run-in with the law, I just try to steer clear of making trouble."

"What does Raoul look like?" Sierra asked.

Camila shrugged. "A punk." She turned into the room and asked them to wait. A moment later, she returned with a photo that looked to be several years old. "This is Inez on her eightieth birthday. The man there is her late son, and the boy standing to his left is Raoul."

Sierra and Pike studied the boy's image: very short dark hair, calculating eyes, gang tattoos, superior sneer. "Do you think it's possible Raoul might have started coming back to this house at night?"

"How could he? I changed the lock."

Pike leaned to check out the front door. "The lock doesn't appear to have been tampered with," he said. "Hang on a second," he added and stepped off the tiny porch, disappearing around the house.

"Can you tell me where Raoul lives?" Sierra asked. "I mean when he's not here."

"I don't know. Maybe with friends, maybe he has a girl once in a while… I seen him hanging out up on Vermont near the Tip Top bar a time or two. You might ask around up there."

Pike showed up again. "The laundry room window has been jimmied open," he said. "Where does Mrs. Ruiz keep her keys?"

Camila gestured at an ornate hanger by the front door from which three or four keys hung. "Right there."

"So you're thinking Raoul might have come in through the laundry?" Sierra asked.

"He'd only have to do it once, take the key, get a copy made, put the original back in place and from then on, he'd be home free." He turned to Camila and added, "Do you want me to secure that window before we go?"

"Would you, please? Guess it's time to change the lock again."

"Are there tools in the garage?"

"I'm not sure." She handed him a key from the little hanger. "You can check."

He left again. Sierra pocketed her phone. "I'm going to have to tell the police everything I learned. I don't want to cause problems for you, but they need to know. They'll send forensics back to process this doorway and everything else and they'll need to talk to Mrs. Ruiz. You and her attorney should be present to help her. May I give them your name and number?"

"Yes," she said with a resigned sigh. "Go ahead."

"And it's probably too late, but don't throw anything away. Just keep all the trash you find in a plastic bag in the garage, in case there's evidence."

IT WAS DARK by the time they got to the Tip Top. The streets were bumper-to-bumper, the sidewalks more or less empty. "There's nowhere to park," Pike said.

"Let me out and I'll ask around about Raoul. You can circle the block. I'll call your cell in a few minutes so you can pick me up." He slowed down the car. She noticed his expression as he scanned the sidewalk. "Don't worry about me, I'll be fine," she added.

"This is a pretty rough part of town," he said.

"Maybe, but I'm no cupcake." She impulsively squeezed his hand before opening the door and getting out of the car. She hurried to the sidewalk to avoid getting hit and prepared herself to enter the dingy bar in front of her.

Before she could take more than a few steps, a group of five men exited the dive and stopped short when they saw her. She avoided eye contact. She could take one on one, but five against one weren't odds she liked.

The men circled her and there was nothing she could do but look into their eyes. That was a sobering experience as she sensed a group mentality concerning single women on "their" turf. A little frisson of fear rippled down her spine that annoyed the heck out of her. She was used to handling herself, but in all truth, she had to admit that the situations in which she usually found herself were a little less raw than this.

She suddenly missed Pike's reassuring presence, but shook off that feeling. Since when did Sierra Hyde depend on a man?

"Anyone here know Raoul Ruiz?" she asked with a resolute effort to exude confidence.

One of the men had a knife scar running across his throat and a superior way of looking down his nose as though detached from what was going on around him. The power and anger radiating from his eyes could probably melt concrete.

He turned in a bored, I've-had-enough-of-this-broad way and walked back inside the bar. The others looked at each other, avoiding eye contact with Sierra, and one by one they followed on Knife Scar's heels, leaving just one guy behind.

Unfortunately, the one who remained was huge. Not tall, really, just a shining example of steroid abuse. He wore a red muscle shirt over bulging abs and pecs and a blue bandanna around his head that almost hid the fact that he had no eyebrows.

"Was it something I said?" she asked Muscle Guy.

"They think you're a cop," he replied.

"Do you?"

"Maybe. Difference is, I don't care."

"Do you know Raoul Ruiz?"

"I might."

"Have you seen him recently?"

"Maybe."

"But you're not going to say."

"Brother don't rat on brother to the cops."

"I'm not a cop. I'm a private detective."

"Not from around here."

"No," she said. "I'm looking for a guy named

Danny Cooke. I thought maybe Raoul would know where he is."

The man stared at her, wheels obviously turning in his head. "What's in it for me?"

"All I got on me. Fifty bucks," she said.

"Beat it, broad," he said loudly and then added in a hushed tone, "Meet me down the alley."

Was Sierra really desperate enough for a lead to follow this behemoth into a dark alley? Turns out the answer was yes.

Chapter Six

Sierra saw her would-be informant's bulging shape lurking behind an industrial Dumpster as she turned down the alley after giving him a head start. She was keenly aware this could go awry and she thought of all the hours spent at the gym. Hopefully she wouldn't have to find out if they paid off.

She stopped a few feet shy of him. "All right, spill it. What can you tell me about Raoul?"

"Dude's a doper."

"And Danny Cooke?"

"Mr. Detroit? Runs a little operation. Weed, crystal, blow, stuff like that."

"When did you see Ruiz last?"

"Earlier this week, driving a blue girlie car."

"Did you see Danny?"

"No."

"Did you speak to Ruiz?"

"Some."

Sierra looked toward the entry of the alley. Her gut was telling her time was running out. "Did he talk about a murder?"

"Murder? No!"

"Did he mention killing someone?"

"What are you talking about? All he said was him and Shorts were leaving town."

"Who is Shorts?"

"A guy."

"Where were they going?"

"Didn't say."

"What's Shorts's real name?"

"Don't know. He just wears shorts all the time." He twitched a little and licked his lips. "Give me the fifty bucks now."

As a lead, this one didn't show much promise. She could tell Detective Hatch about it, though, and maybe he could locate this Shorts person. It all seemed like a long shot.

Suddenly a voice came from behind them. Sierra hadn't heard anyone approaching, but she whirled around to find Knife Scar pointing a gun at her. His gaze flicked from her to Muscle Guy. "How long you been squealing to the cops?"

Sierra doubted that pointing out the difference between a police offer and a private detective would afford her any latitude in her current situation. She stood trapped between two men and knew her chances of outrunning either of them weren't good even without the added factor of the gun.

"Listen, dude, I didn't tell her nothing," the walking muscle insisted.

Knife Scar ignored him. "I'm trying to think of the best way to kill you both. There are so many options." He pointed the gun at his friend's head, then lowered it to aim at Sierra's gut. "I kind of like the thought of starting with you."

With her mind racing for a way out of this, she came up blank. If he moved closer she might have a chance to disarm him. Sure. Probably not, but it was all she could think of. Before she could figure out how to close the distance between them, he was suddenly flying through the air. With a thud, he landed on his back five feet away.

Pike moved quickly to stand over him, jaw tight, fists rolled. He kicked the guy in the side and hauled him to his feet, twisted his arm behind his back and slammed him against the building on the other side of the alley. He took the gun from his hand and pressed it against the guy's thick neck.

Sierra swallowed the last few minutes of terror as Pike kept the guy pinned against the building. The sound of heavy breathing was about all she could hear, but she knew that sooner or later, this guy's buddies would come looking for him and they would be sorely outnumbered. She looked around to see that her informant had fled.

Pike looked into her eyes. "You through with him?"

She thought of trying to question him and decided she'd pushed her luck as far as she wanted to. She nodded and then thought twice and stopped him. She reached into her pocket and produced several plastic cable ties. "Tools of the trade," she said. While Pike held him at gunpoint she tied his hands together. They walked the thug over to the Dumpster, threw back the lid and forced the man to climb into the garbage, where he stumbled to keep upright. Pike pushed him down and slammed the lid. They fled down the alley to the echo of his bellowing.

Once out on a street, they sprinted a couple of blocks to the rental. Pike locked the confiscated weapon in the trunk and they took off without looking back.

BY THE TIME they got to their hotel the adrenaline had started to wear off. "I'm ordering room service," she announced outside her door. "You're welcome to join me."

"That's the best offer I've had today."

"Well, you did waltz into that alley in the nick of time. The least I can do is feed you." She leaned back against her door and ran a finger along his chin. He had a truly delightful face, serious, sexy, playful, his expressions charming and fascinating. "Anything in particular you want?"

"You," he said.

She smiled. "Give me forty-five minutes."

"Is that a promise?"

"I'll let you know in forty-five minutes."

SIERRA SAT DOWN at the table and took out her cell phone, annoyed to see her hand shake. The scene in the alley might have ended differently if Pike hadn't come looking for her. It might have also played out differently if she'd been armed, but she hadn't left New York with the intention of having to shoot anyone.

Tess answered with palatable anticipation. "Sierra? Did you find him?"

"No," Sierra said gently.

"Not even his—his body?"

"Not even his body." She took a deep breath. "Tess, I need you to be very honest with me, okay?"

There was a pause before Tess replied. "I have been."

"Don't get offended. Just answer a couple of questions. Were you and Danny arguing the night he died?"

"Yeah. He could be a jerk. It was no big deal."

"He wouldn't want to scare you, would he?"

"What do you mean?"

"I mean that your car is missing. Could he have faked the shooting—"

"No! What a thing to say. He would never do that to me! Whoever killed Danny has my car."

"Okay. Is it possible you went to that house another time and—"

"No!"

"Let me finish. Is it possible you remember that house for another reason?"

"No!"

"Had you been drinking or doing drugs?"

There was silence for a heartbeat, then a sigh. "I had a shot of brandy, maybe two. I was getting a cold and Danny said it would help."

Sierra reflected for a second. The girl weighed less than a hundred pounds, but a couple of shots, if that's all it really was, wasn't enough to cause her to hallucinate a murder. "Okay, is it possible Danny was shot but not killed?"

This time the answer was even slower to come. "No," she said, but for the first time, there was a note of uncertainty in her voice. "I thought he was dead. He was so still."

"But you had no time to check him, right?"

"I had to go," Tess said, her voice shaking. "The other man had a gun. I was—I was...scared."

"Okay, okay. Calm down. I'm not done looking. We'll be home tomorrow night, okay?"

"Okay."

"It might be late so you don't have to wait up."

"Okay. But I will."

"I know. Are you sleeping?"

"Some."

"Good." They hung up a minute or two later and Sierra sat there to steady her nerves for a moment before calling Grace's phone and filling her in on the situation.

"Don't you worry. I'll make sure she has a warm glass of milk before bed. She'll be fine," Grace said. "Her cold is getting better and I heard her humming today."

As Sierra went in to take a shower she felt pretty sure Tess wasn't humming now. Some big sister she was turning out to be.

SHOWERED, FRESHLY SHAVED and whistling, Pike knocked on Sierra's door. She opened it quickly, and his breath caught. Her red hair was damp again and combed straight back from her face. She wore a slender grass-green kimono trimmed in pink, belted at the waist, plunging at the neckline. The diamond in her neck-lace rested in the hollow of her throat. It was the only jewelry he'd ever seen her wear.

Every single time he saw her, she seemed to seep a little deeper into his pores. "You look amazing," he said.

She smiled. "I haven't had time to get dressed yet."

"Don't hurry on my account," he told her.

She smiled again. "I have an idea."

"I have an idea, too," he said, and took her hands. "It's been forty-seven minutes, you know."

"Mine is about Raoul Ruiz," she said as he pulled her against his chest. He kissed her neck, pushing aside the damp hair, inhaling her.

"Mine isn't," he said. He found her mouth and kissed her. She was so soft and warm and welcoming. He kissed her over and over again, his body scream-ing with anticipation. He'd never wanted a woman the way he wanted her. "You are driving me crazy," he whispered against her ear.

She pulled away from him and looked into his eyes. "Oh, Pike. Are you sure? I can't promise you anything—"

"I'm not asking for promises," he interrupted. "All I want is the here and now."

"Are you sure?" she asked as she cupped his face in her hands and kissed his lips. Her half-closed eyes made his breath catch. "Are you positive?" she added, her lips brushing his cheekbone, his temple.

He lowered his head and kissed her throat. Was

he positive? Hell, no. But he was certain that he was willing to take his chances. There was no other option. He could no more stay away from her than indefinitely hold his breath. The future would just have to take care of itself. "Trust me," he said.

There was a knock on the door and they looked at each other. "I'll get it," he said, and reluctantly released his grip on her arms. A waiter rolled a small table into the room and asked if he could set things up for them. Pike signed the bill, handed the kid a twenty and told him they'd take care of it themselves.

He turned his back on the covered trays. His growing hunger couldn't be sated with food. He went back to Sierra and led her to the bed. "Dinner is going to be late," he said, sliding the kimono down over her shoulder, kissing the exposed skin.

She raised his head and stared into his eyes. "This is all happening so fast," she said.

"I feel like I've known you my entire life," he whispered as he sat on the bed and pulled her beside him. He continued to kiss her throat as he cupped her silk-covered breast.

"I've never known anyone like you," she whispered.

"I'm just a cowboy," he said.

"I'm not talking about that," she murmured. "I'm talking about your heart."

"Currently beating off the charts because of you," he murmured as he slipped the kimono farther down her arm and the belt gave way. He'd never seen or touched a more sensational, creamy, beautiful woman in his life. Her breasts were firm but soft, her stomach flat, hips flaring from a small waist. It took her about thirty seconds to tear off his clothes before they fell together back on the bed. For a moment, he paused, just looking at her face, devouring her beauty, and then she touched him, and after that, everything happened at once.

She was everywhere. Under him, on top of him, seemingly insatiable, arousing parts of him in ways he'd never expected. He strove to be the best lover he'd ever been and then he forgot to worry about it and it seemed she did, too. Instead, they stopped being two people and became one, perfectly in sync, both giving, both taking until the climactic moment that culminated in the beginning of the rest of his life.

He knew he shouldn't think like that. He did so, anyway. Thoughts were private and free. It was uttering them that exacted a price.

At last they lay spent, arms and legs entangled, her head resting on his shoulder. He ran his fingers up and down her arm. He couldn't believe she was lying here with him, that for this moment, she was his.

"You okay?" she asked.

"Almost."

She tilted her head back to look at him and smiled. "You are something else."

"The feeling is mutual."

"No, I mean it. I've never been with a man who was more sure of who and what he is. It's spellbinding. It's fascinating."

He kissed her succulent lips and knew he would never grow tired of the feel and scent of her.

"You hungry?" he asked after a while.

"Getting there. I need to make a call first."

"Tess?"

"No, I called her after we got back today. Now I need to call Camila, Mrs. Ruiz's housekeeper." Her voice sounded anything but businesslike, more sleepy and contented than exacting. "It just occurred to me that she might know Shorts's real name or know where he lives. She may be able to give us a lead to follow tomorrow."

"The intrepid private eye, always at work," he said, sitting up.

She smiled at him. "Not always," she said, and pulled him back down beside her. "Where do you think you're going?" she whispered while nibbling his ear. Her breasts felt weighty and soft against his arm.

"Nowhere," he said, smoothing the hair away from her forehead and kissing her eyelids. "Nowhere at all."

BETWEEN ONE THING and another, Sierra didn't get around to calling Camila Sanchez until morning, while Pike took a shower in his own room. After grabbing coffee and bagels in the lobby, they slid back into the rental. Pike took the wheel again.

"Head east toward Victorville," Sierra told him as she showed him the map on her phone.

He waited until commuter traffic thinned out before saying much. "Okay, tell me what Camila said."

"She knows Shorts because he's one of the punks who hangs out with Raoul. His sister lives on a piece of property this side of Victorville. It's about two hours from here, maybe more with traffic. She wasn't sure what the woman's name is, but she knows Shorts taps her when he needs cash. And if he was traveling, he would need cash, right?"

"Sounds reasonable. How are we supposed to find her?"

"We look for an auto-wrecking place this side of the city."

California had endured a drought for the past few years. Pike was used to the unending vistas of the plateau at home, and in this way, the golden, rolling near-desert struck a familiar chord. Not that the scenery mattered. Being anywhere with Sierra by his side was far better than being anywhere else without her. Even driving out into the desert in a rental car became something of a joyful event with her along. He warned himself he was falling too hard and too fast. He reminded himself of the ground rules: ultimate termination of the relationship. And then he glanced over at her, her face half covered with sunglasses, her pink lips spread into a smile, and he knew all the warnings in the world were inadequate.

"What's the plan, boss?" he asked as they neared their destination.

"We look for a bunch of old cars. Camila says

the sister's husband owned a wrecking yard before he ran his motorcycle into the side of a semitruck."

They drove until they hit the beginning of the city and then they were downtown. "We must have come too far," Sierra said.

"Look up auto-wrecking places on your cell."

"I did. There's nothing listed back the way we came. But Camila said it was before the town. We have to go back."

He turned around and they retraced their route. When they figured they were too far away, they turned again. "It must be off the road," Pike said. "Look for anything suspicious."

Five miles back toward Victorville, Sierra suddenly said, "What was that? Turn around, go back."

He did as she asked and pulled over on a dirt road to find a sculpture he'd been mildly aware of the other two times they'd passed it by. Up close and standing still, he could now see it had been created by welding together old car parts. It was hard to tell what it was supposed to be, but a plastic sign from the hardware store tacked onto the base said Closed. Pike lifted the corner of the sign and discovered it covered another one: Mac's Place.

"Doesn't sound much like an auto-wrecking yard," he said.

"This has to be it. Camila said the sister's husband died about two years ago. I guess she closed the place down. We'll see if she can tell us anything about Raoul."

They drove for a half mile before coming across

a tall chain-link fence surrounding a scattering of abandoned cars that quickly turned into a sea of windshields twinkling in the sunlight. At the hub of this chaos sat a faded aqua double-wide trailer backed by a series of sheds, barns and workshops. Everything had a deserted air except for the trailer, from which they could hear the muted sound of music when they stepped out of the car.

It was much cooler here than in LA—probably no more than forty degrees. Access to the double-wide was by way of a ramp. Their knocks went unanswered until the shrill bark of a dog heralded the sudden opening of the door by a woman in a wheelchair. A small terrier darted out and ran around their legs while the woman spoke, but who could hear a word she said? She adroitly wheeled herself back into the room and switched off a CD player. The sudden silence was pierced only by the yapping dog.

"Olive, shush," the woman said.

The dog immediately stopped barking, trotted back inside the trailer and jumped onto the woman's lap. Dog and owner looked a lot alike: both smallish, both dark blond and both sporting dark, soulful eyes.

"Are you an auto-wrecking business?" Sierra asked.

"Used to be, kind of. Only if Mac had heard you call this place that, he would have had issues. He thought of it more as a reclamation center for dead cars. Anyway, didn't you see the sign? Don't tell me it blew away again. I'm not open."

"Your sign is there but we're not here to ask about cars," Sierra replied. She introduced herself and Pike.

"I'm Polly MacArthur," the woman said. "What can I do for you?"

"We're here because we're trying to get a lead on the whereabouts of a man named Raoul Ruiz. We heard your brother, Shorts, knows him."

"Listen," she said, "ever since my Mac skid his bike under that truck and put me in this chair for the rest of my life, Shorts, aka Dwayne, has been conning me for drug money. This last time he came, he was with a guy I didn't know. Dwayne said he'd conned this man for a ride because his truck was dead in the water. Big surprise. It hasn't run good since Mac is no longer around to tinker on it. Anyway, this time Dwayne didn't ask for cash."

"He just came for a visit?"

"Hell, no," she said with a laugh. "Dwayne isn't exactly a conversationalist. He told me he knew this dude who's rebuilding a 1968 Mustang. He said he remembered Mac had an old wrecked one out on the lot somewhere. He wanted to go take parts off the car and sell them to his pal. Maybe he was embarrassed to beg money off his crippled sister with another guy sitting a few yards away, I don't know. What I do know is it's by far the most enterprising idea Dwayne's ever had, so I said sure, why not, knock yourself out."

"Did you get a good look at this other man?"

"No. He never got out of the car. He kept his face averted, but I could tell he was listening to our conversation."

"Did you notice any tattoos?" Sierra asked, thinking back to the photo Camila had showed them. Raoul Ruiz had several tattoos.

She thought for a second. "Yeah, now that you mention it. He had his arm outside the car and he was wearing a tank. There was a sun, I think. You know, a circle with flames shooting out. I couldn't see what was in the middle."

"When were your brother and this other man here?"

"About five days ago."

"Have you heard from your brother since then?"

"No, but I don't expect to. He'll come around again when he runs low on money."

"So they took the parts and left?"

"Yeah."

"Did your brother mention a car trip he and the other guy might take?"

"Those two on a trip together? That just defies imagination, sorry."

"Okay. How long were they out in the yard?"

"Must have been about thirty minutes. I didn't even know they'd left until Olive barked and I opened a window to see the blue car taking off down the road, kicking up a cloud of dust in its wake. They didn't even stop at the house."

"Did you expect them to?" Pike asked.

"It would have been a decent thing to do," she said. "I guess Dwayne got what he was after, but they left without returning the key or locking the gate behind them."

"Could you tell what kind of car it was?"

She laughed. "You aren't married to a guy like Mac for twelve years without picking up on stuff like that. It was a sky-blue Chevy Volt, this year's model or last."

"Did they walk out on the lot or drive?" Sierra asked.

"They drove. There are almost five acres crammed with old wrecks. Nobody goes out there anymore but I figure the roads must be in pretty good shape."

"May we drive out there, too?" Sierra asked.

Polly tilted her head and regarded them for a second. "Is Dwayne in trouble?"

"I don't know," Sierra said. "He's simply our only link to Raoul Ruiz and we need to ask him a few questions concerning a third man named Danny Cooke. And yes, Raoul had access to a blue Chevy Volt."

"The Cooke name is familiar for some reason," Polly said.

"He's a penny-ante drug dealer."

"Figures. Sure, go ahead. Like I said, the gate is unlocked."

Chapter Seven

"Talk about a needle in a haystack," Pike said as they drove along a road that threaded its way between two rows of every kind of abandoned, rusted, wrecked vehicle known to man, then doubled back and started again going the other direction in a series of parallel tracks.

"Well, I know what a Mustang looks like," she said. "My dad used to drive one."

"Do you really think they were looking for car parts out here?" Pike asked.

"No. What I think they were doing is stowing Danny Cooke's body in one of these cars and then continuing their trip to who knows where."

"But which car?"

"The police will have to go through them all," she said. "They can use a cadaver dog. Anyway, we don't have time. We need to be back at the airport by what time?"

"Check-in is at five. We can't leave this place any later than about twelve thirty. We still have to drop by Mona's house to pick up the bags she promised to pack with Tess's things." At least he hoped she'd actually done it. He made a mental note to call her to make sure.

"We also have to deliver the guy in the alley's weapons to Detective Hatch and try to explain what might have happened to Danny," Sierra said.

The weed-infested road looped through the aisles of cars like a line at a Disneyland attraction. They reached the far end of it, admired a cactus standing on the other side of the seven-foot chain-link fence topped with a row of razor wire and turned around. On the way back Pike suddenly stopped the car. "There's a Mustang," he said, gesturing at a pale green rusted-out coupe that hadn't been visible going the other direction.

He opened the rental door and got out. Tess did the same. "What are you doing?"

"There are actually four or five Mustangs in various states of disrepair," he said, surveying the aged metal hulks in front of him. A couple barely looked like cars. "I don't get the feeling Shorts and Raoul are the smartest guys in the world. What if they actually used the Mustang as the dump site?" He started making his way through the car parts to get to the first almost-complete car that was missing all its doors, its engine hood and both fenders. He scanned it quickly and shook his head.

Moving along, he paused and sniffed the air. "Sierra, do you smell something terrible?"

She joined him. "I know that smell. That's rotting flesh."

"It's not that strong. Could be a coyote or a stray dog," he said.

They both stared at the green Mustang. Someone had put a rusted wheel rim off a big truck on top of the trunk sometime in the past. As Pike lifted it off, he heard Sierra warn him not to, but it was too late. With the weight removed, the trunk sprang open. Both he and Sierra recoiled at once but not before the horrible image of a dead man wearing red shorts burned itself into their eyeballs. Pike caught the glistening human-sized shape of black plastic wrapped with duct tape underneath the dead man.

Holding his breath, he closed the trunk and replaced the rim. He grabbed Sierra as he backed away. The trunk was sealed again, but the putrid odor hung heavy in the dry air, and they drove away with the smell of death in their nostrils.

SEVEN HOURS LATER, they boarded their plane. Pike had upgraded their tickets to first class and they sank into recliner-like comfort. He was thrilled when the sheriff had allowed them to return to Idaho after an afternoon of answering questions and explaining what they'd seen and who they'd talked to within the past twenty-four hours.

Poor Polly MacArthur had been called upon to identify her brother's remains. "Looks like Dwayne helped Ruiz move Cooke's body to the wreck, then Ruiz knocked him out," Sheriff Keith Rogers told them. He sounded like he was fresh from Texas. "The ME says it appears he was shot at close range with a foam rubber cushion of some kind buffering the sound. Danny Cooke was wrapped in the plastic, his empty wallet thrown in for good measure. We're searching the country for Raoul Ruiz and the blue Chevy. I talked to Detective Hatch in LA like you asked me to. He said to tell you your sister needs to come back ASAP and tell her story in her own words."

"Ruiz probably ditched the Chevy knowing Polly MacArthur could identify it," Sierra said.

"Probably."

"Oh, and Polly mentioned a tattoo on Ruiz's arm."

"Yeah, she told me about it," he said, checking his notes. "Ruiz is a wanna-be member of a gang called Border Brothers. It consists of undocumented immigrants, usually from the same area of Mexico. The tattoo is a sun with an Aztec god in the middle and an acronym… Anyway, he was actually born in LA, so I'm supposing he got the tat as a sign of solidarity. Most likely it differed slightly when viewed up close and personal."

"Wasn't it kind of risky leaving Dwayne's rotting corpse in his own sister's backyard, so to say?" Pike asked.

"She hasn't been out there since her husband's death," the sheriff replied. "It's cool enough to keep the smell down for a while."

They landed after an uneventful flight during which they held hands and attempted to let go of the day's anxieties. Upon landing, they were greeted by blowing snow as they crossed the parking lot to Pike's SUV.

Two and a half hours later, they rattled over the cattle guard onto Hastings land, but it was a distinctly muted sound. Pike pointed out tracks of another vehicle that were quickly being covered by the falling snow. Someone else in the family must be out and about. Pike was glad he'd put studded snow tires on his vehicle.

As always, he felt the pull of this ranch deep in his soul, and to be coming home with Sierra by his side seemed to fill crevices he hadn't even known existed. Another cautionary warning flashed in his brain, but he stuffed it into a corner with all the rest.

"Do you think the advance documentary crew is still here?" Sierra asked. They had just passed the road to Pike's barn and the desire to veer off in that direction was impossible to deny. He hadn't made love to her since that morning and all he truly wanted in his heart of hearts was to take her into his bed in his own house. He wanted memories of her there, visions he could call on when the day came for her to leave.

But his priority right now had to center on Tess. He'd called his father and told him of their grisly discovery and asked that Tess not be told until he and Sierra were there to do it, but until then, not to let her out of their sight. She had to know the facts because they would soon be public knowledge and she had to be prepared. There was a cold-blooded killer on the run, a man who had murdered a friend he'd enlisted to help him get rid of the body of his drug dealer. Would a man like that leave an eyewitness like Tess alive to talk about him? As far as Pike could see, Dwayne's sister was lucky Raoul hadn't decided to eliminate her, as well. The fact that he hadn't shown his face probably saved her life.

"Hey, over there," Sierra said gently as she tapped his thigh. "I lost you."

"Sorry, I was thinking," he admitted. "But in answer to your question, I doubt the crew will still be here. A storm like this will be around for a few days. We're likely to lose power. I imagine they hightailed it out before it hit."

However, the LOGO van was still parked by the main house. The snow was deeper down in this little valley by the river, and the landscape had turned white. After just two days in seventy-degree weather, the twenty degrees they faced getting out of the SUV felt like a walk-in freezer.

Though it was almost midnight, they found Grace in the kitchen, sitting at the counter working a crossword puzzle, and she looked up when they entered. Disappointment flashed across her face and the pit of Pike's stomach fell. "What's wrong?" he said.

"I was hoping you were your father."

"Why? Where's Dad?"

"He and your brothers rode out to find those television people, who went to shoot pictures of the falling snow before dinner and never came back."

"What? In a storm?"

"We couldn't talk them out of it. They saddled up and rode off like they were the characters in an old Western. Your dad has been gone for hours now."

"Did you call him?" Pike said as he took out his cell."

"Of course. We've been in sporadic communication, but you know what reception is like out here— iffy at best. Last I heard they were going to go film some cattle hunkering down for the storm because Frankie said that's what the cameraman wanted to shoot. But who knows where they are now. I'm sure they're fine—"

Pike's phone rang and that startled all of them. He glanced at the screen and answered. "Frankie?"

His brother's voice was broken. Mountains, weather, valleys and inadequate cell towers all contributed to communication issues they were used to, but this was especially frustrating. "Speak up," Pike said and listened. The only words he was pretty sure he caught before the connection died were *injury* and *tree*.

He related this information and then Grace's phone rang. "It's Harry," she announced and answered immediately. Her smile turned into a frown as she clicked off the phone. "The call was dropped," she said and immediately started texting him.

"I'm going after them," Pike said.

"Do you think that's a good idea?" Grace asked, but he could tell by the way her eyes lit that she was yearning for him to do just that.

"I heard the word *tree* and the only tree around

here those documentary people were interested in was the hanging tree. And I'm pretty sure I heard *injury*. I'm going to hook the trailer up to the biggest snowmobile and head out. Grace, could you get the emergency medical kit and maybe heat up a couple thermoses of something hot to drink?"

"Of course," she said and hurried out of the kitchen to get the kit.

Pike turned to Sierra. "I hate to leave you."

"I understand, it's okay. I wonder where Tess is."

"Grace will know." He took her hands and kissed her fingers. "I'll be back in a few hours. You can sleep here or go back to my place."

"I'll stay here," she said. "Tess said she'd wait up."

"Okay."

There was more he wanted to say because she had made him into a giant sap in the last three days. Instead he stared into her green eyes. "You're going to tell her what we found?"

She nodded. "She has to know. There are plans to make."

"Give her a while to digest everything first, okay?" he said.

She smiled and squeezed his hand. "Yes, I know. I will."

He kissed her again, turned away and walked back outside, but not before stopping in the mud-room to borrow the appropriate cold-weather gear and a flashlight from his dad's supply. Outfitted in gloves, a hat and a heavy jacket, he made his way to the equipment barn.

"SHE'S UPSTAIRS," GRACE said when Sierra inquired about Tess. "Lily went up there hours ago with Charlie and Tess went with them, saying she wanted to text friends and read. Her cold has still got her down, but something else is on her mind. She's been very quiet since your call, but I couldn't get her to open up."

"I know she's going to take the news of Danny's death hard," Sierra said.

Grace screwed the top on the thermos. "Of course. Poor dear."

"May I ask why Lily lives here and not with Chance," Sierra added. "I know it's none of my business, but I'm curious. It's obvious they're crazy about one another."

"Yes, they are, but there's Charlie to consider. His father...died...not too long ago. Lily and Chance are getting married this fall, but until then, Lily asked if she and Charlie could live here with me and Harry, and we were delighted to say yes." She handed Sierra the last thermos of soup, which Sierra tucked in a basket with the other two and a stack of tin cups. "There are some blankets in the chest in the downstairs bedroom. Will you get them?"

"Of course," Sierra said and did as asked, but her thoughts were frantically running from the barn with Pike to upstairs with Tess. She felt split in two pieces. She took the basket of broth and the blankets out to the barn to give to Pike, who tucked them in the trailer before folding her in his arms. "I'll be back," he said, brushing her hair away from her face and kissing her forehead.

His embrace was difficult to leave. Never had another human being's arms created such a conflicting oasis of sanctuary charged with awareness. "Be careful."

He kissed her. "Good luck with Tess."

"Thanks, I'm going to talk to her now." He turned to the machine and she added, "I want to thank you."

He turned back to her, his expression surprised. "Thank me? For what?"

She reached up and touched his cheek and shook her head.

"Sierra," he said, lifting her chin so their gazes connected. "Thank me for what?"

"For today," she finally said.

"Today? If I hadn't opened that trunk—"

"Then I would have. Not for that. For being there, for being with me, for letting me be...I don't know, me. You know?"

He smiled at her and pulled her to his chest.

"I know you have other things to think about right now," she added. "Lord knows, I do, too. But I just—"

He effectively cut this speech short by kissing her again. "We'll finish this later, okay?"

She nodded. "Okay."

"Because I'll be back."

"I know."

He stared into her eyes for a long moment. What did he see? She wasn't sure. She just knew what she saw in his and it shook her down to her soul. A moment later, he started the snowmobile and a moment after that he was gone.

She retrieved her suitcase from his vehicle on the way back to the house and carried it inside, where Grace was just finishing wiping down the drain boards. "The downstairs bedroom is empty now if you and Tess want to use it," she said.

"Thanks," Sierra said, still distracted. She figuratively straightened her shoulders and shook off the last few minutes. "If it's okay with you, I'm going to go talk to Tess and then maybe I'll catch up with some work on my laptop in the room with the fireplace. I don't think I could actually sleep."

"I know what you mean. I have some darning to do so I'll be in there, too." She laughed and added, "Don't look at me that way, young lady, people still do darn good woolen socks, you know."

"I didn't know," Sierra said with a smile. "But I do now."

Sierra went to the room where she'd seen Tess only three days before and found it dark. She peeked inside and discerned a shape beneath the blanket. Obviously, Tess had fallen asleep so Sierra closed the door but didn't latch it. There was no way she was going to wake her sister to tell her about Danny. Sierra knew the hard way that getting upsetting news the moment you awaken sucked big-time. She'd learned about her father's heart attack with an early morning phone call from his girlfriend.

A door opened across the hall and a very pretty,

small woman in her midtwenties with light brown hair peeked out. Lily, Chance's fiancée, smiled. "Are they back yet?" she whispered.

"No," Sierra said.

"I heard something outside."

"That was Pike riding out on a snowmobile. He got a call from Frankie. He thinks someone may be injured at a place called the hanging tree."

"One of our men?"

For a second, Sierra just stared at her, uncertain how to respond, and then her head cleared. "You mean one of the Hastingses? No, I didn't get that feeling, but really, I'm not sure now that you ask."

"I sure hope not."

"Yeah," Sierra said. "Me, too."

THE QUICKEST WAY to the plateau was a trail beside a stream that ran down the hillside behind the house. But that trail was accessible by foot or horseback alone, not with a snowmobile and certainly not one pulling a seven-foot-long trailer. He would have to use the roads, although he could cut through a field or two to shave off some time.

It was likely his father and brothers would do their best to build a fire to use for warmth and as a beacon. His cell needed a charge after the busy day he'd just had, but it should have a call or two left in it. He'd save it for the chance that he'd misunderstood Frankie's garbled message and went to the wrong place.

The ride was grueling. The snow was almost two

feet deep in places, piling up against fences. The cattle were mostly in more protected fields and were likely staying in the brush to escape the snow; they could take care of themselves, although tomorrow the task of delivering hay would begin in earnest. It was the city slickers he needed to worry about now.

An hour later, so cold he'd lost most of the feeling in his legs, he spotted the glow of an open flame. As he drew nearer, he could see a fire had been built under the partial protection of the old hanging tree. Indistinct shapes surrounded it.

He stopped shy of the tree and for a second he just sat there looking at the scene in front of him.

Cast in the subdued glow of struggling flames and overlaid with blowing snow, things looked surreal—almost like a still shot from an old film. His father and two of his brothers stood at the perimeter of the light, firearms drawn. Their demeanor telegraphed watchfulness. The crew huddled close to the warmth. One was prone on the ground, the camera guy was shooting pictures and two leaned against the mammoth tree that would become the object of their film. The reins of the three horses his dad and brother had ridden were tied to the exposed curve of a gnarled root. The animals looked appropriately cold and dejected as only horses could look when they'd rather be somewhere else, say a cozy barn. There was no sign of the crew's four horses and Pike hoped they had the sense to make their way home.

"What the hell happened here?" Pike asked as he approached Frankie on foot.

"Someone shot off a gun," Frankie said.

That stopped Pike in his tracks. "A gun? Out here?"

"Yep. They seem to think it's their old employee out on a rampage."

"But you don't?"

Frankie shook his head. "Seems unlikely."

"Anyone hurt?"

"Gary. As I understand it, they were on their way back from filming a group of miserable cold cows when they stopped here to get some shots of the snow falling through the branches of the hanging tree. Oliver said they were all on horseback, just kind of hanging out discussing things, when they heard a shot fired from somewhere close by. Gary's horse reared up and dumped Gary out of the saddle. He tried to brace his fall and injured his left shoulder. Don't know if it's a break or what. In fact, every last man was thrown to the ground except for Ogden, who managed to stay mounted until his horse jumped a gully, then he had to walk back here to find out about the others. We showed up after they got Gary settled, but we need a transport to get Gary back to the house without further injuring him."

"What about the gunman?"

"Dad and Chance rode around looking for any evidence of another person out here, but the storm had covered all tracks by then and it's just getting nastier by the second."

"There's no one around right now to be shooting anything," Pike said. "Not on this land. And who goes out target practicing in a blizzard? Did you find a bullet or a casing?"

"No."

"Is it possible they heard branches crack and thought it was a gun?"

"Anything is possible, although these guys aren't idiots. Anyway, it's academic right now. We need to get them out of here."

Pike caught his brother's arm as he turned. "First tell me how Daisy is. I didn't have a chance to stop by the house. No puppies, yet I assume?"

"Not yet. By the way, how do you keep her off the sofa?"

"I don't," Pike said.

They distributed the hot broth Grace had sent and set about transporting Gary to the trailer hooked to the back of the snowmobile. The ride to the ranch would need to be slow because of his injuries and because the machine would be hauling several people and the weather just kept deteriorating.

He'd tried numerous times to phone someone at the house. He knew Sierra's phone didn't work out here, but Grace's and Lily's both did. No one responded to calls or texts. Not being able to reach anyone combined with the mysterious shot that had spooked the horses created a restless unease that raced along Pike's spine.

He approached Chance. "You know about Tess's boyfriend, don't you?"

"Yeah. Dad told me."

Pike knew it defied imagination to think that Raoul Ruiz, a city boy by all accounts, had driven to Idaho, found this ranch, bought himself a rifle, made his way out into the snow and taken a shot at a film crew—how would he know they were even here?—on the brink of a well-publicized winter storm all to get Tess alone with no one but other women to defend her. It wasn't impossible, however, and since no other explanation popped to mind, that's what he was left with.

If that was the case, Raoul hadn't figured on Sierra Hyde, who Pike didn't doubt was no slouch with a firearm. Neither was Grace, for that matter. "Maybe her boyfriend's killer is behind this," he told Chase.

"I hadn't thought about that," Chance said doubtfully.

"I know it's far-fetched, but no more so than a vengeful ex-employee running around on unfamiliar ground taking shots. I want to get back to the house. If I take your horse and go down the hill, I can be there in half the time."

"Take Dad's, I'm going with you. Lily and Charlie are in that house, too, and weirder things have happened around here."

A few minutes later, Pike and Chance headed across the plateau to find the trail that would lead them down the hill to the oasis in the U-shaped bend of the river, where their father's house had been built decades before.

Pike didn't know if Chance's heart was lodged somewhere in his throat, but he knew his was.

Chapter Eight

After Grace finally had a short conversation with Harry, she fell asleep in her chair. Sierra fielded a few emails, promising existing and potential clients she'd return to New York as soon as she could. But there was still the matter of Tess and another trip to Los Angeles to take into account. Savannah Papadakis had kind of disappeared and Sierra was secretly relieved. She'd deal with all that later.

Sierra closed her eyes. The day had been long and grueling and she was tired down to her bones. Her thoughts got more and more scattered until, in a haze of darkness, a man ran toward her on a city street. She attempted to step out of his way but he veered to intercept her and knocked her to the ground. Breathless, she looked at him as he sat on top of her. He now wore a Giants football uniform and he was screaming at the top of his lungs. She couldn't understand what he was saying because of his helmet, so she snatched it off his head. Old, bald and wizened, he stared directly into her eyes. "You idiot," he growled and disappeared.

Her eyes flew open. She took a couple of deep breaths as she reoriented herself. The dream had seemed so real, the insult more like a warning. The fire still crackled on the grate; Grace still slept in her chair. The wind outside rattled tree limbs against the windows, but that was the only sound. Sierra checked the time on her laptop and saw she'd only slept a few minutes. Was it the residue of her dream that made her uneasy or something else?

Without thinking it through, she put aside her equipment and got out of the chair. She climbed the stairs and walked down the hall to Pike's old bedroom, where she'd seen Tess asleep when she first got back. As she approached the door, the angry bald man flashed in her brain.

She pushed open the door. Nothing had changed. There was still a bump in the bed, the lights were still off, the room was deathly silent.

Silent.

Where was the sound of a sleeping human with a head cold?

She flicked on the overhead light and approached the bed, realizing way before she threw back the covers that the shape she'd assumed was her sister was in reality two pillows under a blanket. There was also a piece of paper and Sierra, struggling not to tremble, sat down and read a hastily scrawled note.

Sierra and Pike,
I heard from Danny! He's alive. He was hurt, but he managed to escape. He's come to see me

but he's afraid he's being followed. He asked
me where we could meet. I thought about the
barn, but now everyone is running around all
worried about those television people so I'm
going to saddle up and meet Danny at the old
mine. He told me not to tell anyone where I
was going but to bring Sierra along because he
wanted to thank her for taking care of me. But
I heard a storm is coming and your plane could
be delayed so I'm leaving this note instead and
going on by myself. I have to see him. He's all
I have. Don't worry about me, okay?
Love you guys, Tess.

For a second, Sierra just sat there, head reeling.
Where was this mine Tess was talking about? She
sprang to her feet and raced downstairs. Her pounding footsteps must have awakened Grace, who was
yawning into her fist when Sierra came into the den.

"Oh, no," Grace said when she met Sierra's gaze.
"Now what?"

"May I use your phone?" Sierra said. "Mine doesn't
work out here and Tess is gone."

Grace handed Sierra the phone as Sierra handed
Grace the note Tess had left. Tess did not respond and
Sierra left a message. She turned to peruse the gun
cabinet. "Do you have the key for this?" she asked.

"It's in the desk drawer," Grace said as she looked
up from the note. "God in heaven. How could I have
missed Tess leaving?"

"It sounds as if she took advantage of the commotion surrounding the guys saddling up and taking off."

"But I was supposed to be looking out for her," Grace lamented. "And who in the world texted the girl?"

"Well, Danny is dead, there's no two ways about that," Sierra said as she snatched the key from the middle drawer and hurried back to the cabinet. "Someone else wanted to get her alone and I'm guessing it's the guy who murdered Danny. His name is Raoul Ruiz. Do you know what mine she's talking about?"

"There's only one and it's in the ghost town. Sierra, you can't go alone. You don't even know where it is."

"You'll tell me."

"We could get Kinsey or Lily—"

Sierra took Grace's hands. "Listen to me. If this is Raoul, who knows what he'll do. Kinsey is pregnant. I am not asking her to go out in this weather. Lily has Charlie to protect and I am not asking her to leave him. They need you at this house just in case. That leaves me. So draw a map while I go change into jeans. Then help me saddle a horse. Can I use the Glock in the cabinet?"

"Take whatever you need. Ammo is in the drawer."

Sierra affected a five-minute change into warmer clothes, then gratefully accepted a borrowed wool jacket and gloves. As Grace saddled the horse, Sierra recalled the photo she'd snapped in Pike's barn, the one of the Hastings Ridge Ranch. Her phone might not get reception, but she could bring up photos. She'd sent the photo to her laptop and now wished she'd thought to study it on that larger screen. Even the smaller version helped orientate her, however, and that would have to do.

"Won't the dogs try to follow me?" she asked Grace as the three animals milled around the horse.

"In this weather? No way, but I'll lock them in the mudroom just to be safe. You be careful, now."

It took two tries for Sierra to swing herself onto the saddle. She'd only ridden a few times in her life, and then during daylight hours on placid horses. This was the craziest thing she'd ever done, she knew that, but she also couldn't think of an alternative.

"Here's a flashlight," Grace said. "This is the map, but I'm no artist like Kinsey. I put a compass heading for when you reach the plateau. If you go out the back gate and head toward the hills and trees, your horse will find the trail and get you up to the plateau. With any luck, you'll run in to the menfolk and one of them will help you. Otherwise, veer off toward the right and just keep going until you get to the old ghost town, then ride all the way to the end. That's where the mine is. And for goodness' sake, be careful or Pike will have my head. I'll send him or someone else along as soon as they return."

"Go inside and arm yourself," Sierra replied. "Keep the doors locked. And you might call Kinsey and tell her the same thing," she added, shoving the gun in her waistband.

She took off into the night, fingers figuratively

crossed, heart racing. Grace had turned on the flood-
lights and that helped her find the gateway to the
creek. And sure enough, the horse began the winding climb on sure feet. The trees overhead slowed
down the snowfall and Sierra held on for dear life
as the path became steeper. Her mind kept racing
to the mine she had to find, and what had become
of Tess, who had not recorded the time on her note.
Who knew how long she'd been gone, but if she'd
left right after the Hastingses had gone looking for
the crew, it had to be hours now, more than enough
time for her to have reached this mine and for Raoul
to have done heaven knows what to her.

It seemed to take forever and then some to reach
level land, and she looked through the falling snow
in an effort to find some sign of life. Disappointed
beyond words—she really had hoped she'd run in to
Pike out here, or if not him, then one of his brothers
or their father—she kept riding, trusting the horse
to know the lay of the land and find footing. Common sense suggested the ground was uneven under
the snow, but the horse kept moving and her gait was
such that Sierra was relatively comfortable in the
saddle. She didn't dare kick the horse into a run because she wasn't sure if she'd be able to stop it. Better to get there in one piece sometime tonight than
risk a broken neck and never arrive at all.

For a girl used to crowded sidewalks and sub-
ways, this lonely night with only one big heavy-
breathing horse and a sky full of snow for company
seemed to stretch into eternity. Using the flashlight,

she checked the compass heading and saw that she was as close to right on as she could get without micromanaging every step. The horse actually seemed to know the way, and Sierra formed a growing admiration for the way the big red beast kept her head down and one foot in front of the other.

Robbed of any landmarks, she had no reference points. They could be walking in giant circles and, if not for the compass, she wouldn't know. Eventually, so cold her teeth had stopped chattering, she felt rather than saw a change and shined the flashlight to the right. A large dark building was discernable through the snow. Eureka! She'd found the ghost town, or at least she assumed she had. The light played over additional shapes and she felt more confident. Soon, spectral buildings appeared on either side of her and she guessed she was riding down Main Street. The road took a curve and then the buildings petered out, and after a while longer, a hillside appeared at the edge of a large clearing that was scattered with hulking pieces of what must be old mining equipment.

In the face of what appeared to be a rocky outcropping, she saw a darker area shaped like an arc. This must be the entrance. Grace had said that it was covered with a locked door, but Sierra saw no evidence of one. Tracks in the snow suggested activity within the last few hours.

"We found it," she whispered through blue lips to the horse. Her numb legs almost collapsed as her feet hit the ground. A sound from close by sent her heart into her throat and she twirled around, flashlight illuminating nothing but snow at first, until a large shape materialized and hastened toward her like a banshee out of a horror film.

She reached for the Glock but paused at the sound of a throaty snort. The apparition turned into a horse, and it came to within a few feet of her then stopped. Its breath shot out in a cloud as it stamped a foot on the snowy ground and whinnied.

Sierra grabbed the reins of the horse's bridle. The animal was still saddled. It seemed likely that this was the horse Tess had ridden to come here, so that must mean she was still in the mine.

She had to wonder: How did a person unfamiliar with this land find his way to the mine? She thought back to the map. She hadn't noticed other roads, but there must have been at least one. Was it reasonable to expect Raoul Ruiz to be able to navigate out here on a night like this? On the other hand, she recalled the tracks in the snow when they got to Hastings land. Who had driven through that gate when everyone on the ranch was either inside a house or out rescuing the film crew on horses?

She led both animals to the opening of the mine because she wasn't sure what else to do with them. What if they were needed for a quick getaway? What if they wandered off to find someplace more hospitable? How would she and Tess get back to the ranch? The flashlight revealed a few boards jutting up through the snow. Presumably, they were all that was left of the door. The light also revealed an iron rod embedded in the rock right outside the entrance. Maybe it had supported the door. She looped the reins around the iron. The horses could stand inside if they wanted or stay outside—their choice. Satisfied with her solution, Sierra shined the light into the mine and took a deep breath.

There weren't too many things that seriously rattled her, but underground cavities were one of them. And somehow, this ancient, abandoned, man-made mine was twice as terrifying as a cave Mother Nature created. She flashed the light around once, trying to orientate herself, knowing she would have to be careful with both noise and light as she got deeper and hopefully closer to Tess.

The mine tunnel was heavily shored with lumber. Were there bats in here? Probably not, since it had been closed until just recently. No wonder it smelled like a grave. On the other hand there might be fissures leading to the surface through which bats could enter. She could almost feel them in her hair—obviously she'd seen too many Scooby-Doo cartoons as a kid.

Sags and even areas where the lumber had failed altogether made piles of dirt and rock. The tunnel itself appeared pretty straight as far as the light penetrated. A railroad-like track ran along the ground.

Sierra took off her hat, shook off the snow, took the Glock from her waistband and turned off the light. Moving as quickly and silently as she could, she kept her gloved hand touching the wall as she progressed. In all the years she'd been an investigator, she'd actually only pulled out her gun once, maybe twice. Guns tended to escalate a problem and were a tool of last resort for her.

But this felt different. This felt like the Old West and it was hard not to juxtapose her present situation with all the old Westerns she'd watched with her father. For a second she thought of those long-ago bank robbers thundering out of town with their loot, a posse not far behind. For the first time it seemed real.

The air quality abruptly changed and the wall disappeared. She chanced the light again. The tunnel had turned and within fifteen feet, the track on the ground split into two and veered off at right angles to each other.

Again she walked in darkness until she felt air all around her. On came the light. She'd been worrying about which track to take, but now she saw that the spur was actually blocked by a cave-in. While that made the choice easier, it also reminded her how fragile this world was.

The clear tunnel began a rapid decline deeper into the earth. She moved slowly, worried that her feet in the thin-soled boots might slip on the pebbles that littered the ground. She kept listening for voices— Tess's or anyone else's for that matter—but the place was eerily silent, the air cold and dank.

The tunnel wall disappeared and she once again used the light. A deep crevice on her right side looked like nature's handiwork and stretched on along the side of the tunnel. The tracks hugged the opposite wall and continued until they disappeared around another turn. She set off once more, this time walking on top of the track to stay far away from the crevice. She strained to hear any sound that signaled a living human being, refusing to even consider the possibility that Tess lay dead up ahead.

At the place where the tunnel turned sharply to the right, she paused. There wasn't a noise to be heard. She had to have light before chancing a change of direction. The tunnel evolved here into a wider cavern. The crevice she'd noticed earlier was still here. There were a couple of empty mining carts and old metal tubs scattered about, as well as additional tunnels branching off what seemed to be this central area. Near the edge of the rift, she spied a pile of rubble consisting of dirt and rotting timbers. Was it the result of another cave-in?

The light illuminated a splotch of red beneath the rubble. Closer examination revealed a red knit hat. If it wasn't the one she'd seen hanging in the ranch mudroom, then it was its twin. Next to it, she found a pink loafer, and her heart sank as she fell to her hands and knees and shone the light into the seemingly bottomless gash in the earth.

She played the light against the opposing wall, which appeared relatively smooth. Then she aimed the light straight down on her side of the chasm. There was a narrow ledge down there, two or three feet wide. Another pink shoe lay amid additional rubble. There was no sign of Tess.

Had she been knocked into the bowels of the earth or had she been taken away from this mine? If the sole purpose was to silence her forever, then her body probably lay down at the bottom of the rift.

As Sierra stared at the pink shoe she heard a sound from behind and turned her head.

"SHE DID WHAT?" Pike said when he and Chance got back to the house. They'd found Grace asleep while sitting at the kitchen counter, a rifle on one side of her and an empty pot of coffee on the other. Hollow-eyed, she'd roused herself as they entered from the mudroom, obviously embarrassed to have been caught napping on guard duty. Chance mumbled that he'd be right back and left the kitchen, headed for the second floor to check on Lily and Charlie.

"Tess left a note," Grace repeated, her eyes moist and her voice gravelly. "She said Danny texted a message asking her and Sierra to meet him. She didn't want to wait for Sierra. She remembered the old mine you'd shown her, so she suggested that to this supposed Danny. In her defense, it was dark and cold out, but the storm hadn't fully hit yet. Anyway, Sierra read the note Tess left and decided to go after her."

"How is Sierra going to get there in this weather and at night?" he asked. "She's never even been there before. And can she actually ride a horse?"

"I think she can do almost anything she puts her mind to," Grace responded and he had to agree. "And as for getting there, she had a map of this ranch on her phone. I gave her compass headings. Frankly, I was hoping she'd meet up with you along the way."

"How long has she been gone?"

"About two hours."

"She must have ridden past the tree while we were still out there. In this weather she could have been thirty feet away."

"This is all my fault," Grace said with tears in her eyes. "I was responsible for watching Tess and I failed."

He patted her shoulder. "You know people can be sneaky when they want to be. It's just as much our fault for not telling Tess the truth about Danny so she wouldn't fall for some con. None of that matters right now. I have to go after them."

"Wait for Chance to go with you," Grace said.

"No time. Tell him to stay here until the others arrive and then come. I'll text when I have an idea where they are."

He rushed into the mudroom, where he reclaimed the shotgun he'd laid aside and grabbed a flashlight from a basket. Out in the barn, he saddled a fresh horse and snagged a coiled rope that hung on a post. Within minutes, he rode back up the creek, following what had turned into a muddy trail.

The trip was a grueling issue of mind over matter. It was three or four in the morning by now and he was exhausted and yet panicked at the same time. The wind had picked up enough to cause the snow to blow almost parallel to the ground. The ghostly moans as it snaked through the old town made the hairs stand up on his neck.

At the mine entrance, he found two saddled horses dragging reins in the snow. At the sight of him and another horse, they made low grunting sounds in their throats. The wild look in their eyes reflected tension and they skittered away from him as the sound of an accelerating engine reached Pike's ears. It had to be a snowmobile leaving via the old road that ran parallel to the town and eventually looped around to the main ranch access road.

He should have waited for Chance. Cursing the fact that he was alone, he rounded up the horses and looped the reins around a piece of equipment. He knew the snowmobile tracks would linger for a while even in this snowfall. He'd have to hope he could find them after making sure Tess and Sierra weren't in need of help.

He looped the coil of rope over one shoulder and his saddlebag over the other, as it contained some emergency supplies, including a flask of water. Wielding the flashlight in one hand and the shotgun in the other, he entered the mine.

It had been absolutely forbidden to enter this place when he was a kid. That hadn't stopped him and his brothers from doing just that, however, and they'd spent many a secret afternoons investigating its tunnels, shafts and the natural underground chambers. He flashed the light and then from memory made his way to the central area, moving swiftly but with caution, unsure what he'd find.

He knew there were natural-occurring fissures and he also knew that deep shafts had been dug decades before to access veins of gold. He remembered where the tunnel branched and discovered a cave-in had more or less sealed the way.

Once again he fought the craziness of the possibility that someone like Raoul Ruiz would orchestrate the chain of events that had occurred this night. True, he didn't know the man, but he knew about him and it seemed implausible. Wasn't he more the walk-up-to-you-and-shoot-you-in-the-face kind of guy? Other explanations evaded him, however. He wasn't satisfied with any answer he could come up with or even the questions. So what? Time to hunker back into rescue mode and stop trying to figure it out.

He found the main cavern empty aside from the tracks and abandoned mining equipment he and his brothers had played on as kids.

A weak light shone on the ground near the edge of a chasm. A flashlight had been dropped next to a pile of rubble. His gut twisted in a knot. People don't abandon a light source in a place as dark and treacherous as this unless they'd been forced to. As he fumbled with the reclaimed flashlight, its weak beam caught something twinkling in the dirt. Kneeling down, he picked up a fine gold chain adorned with a single diamond pendant. He battled the creeping ache that he'd never see Sierra alive again and buttoned the necklace into his shirt pocket.

Further investigation of the rubble revealed dirt and boards and a red knit hat caught under a rafter as though it had been knocked off its wearer. There was no sign of a body under the rubble. A pink shoe lay abandoned a few feet away. He wasn't sure about the cap, but he knew the shoe belonged to Tess.

When they'd been young boys, he and his brothers had marched fearlessly through this mine. Now he moved with caution and determination. He lay on his belly and scanned the ledge below with his flashlight. A woman lay facedown too near the fragile lip for comfort. The light glowed on her red hair, leaving little doubt as to her identity.

"Sierra!" he yelled.

For a moment he was sure she moved, but in the next instant he realized it was an illusion caused by the trembling of his own hand as he grasped the flashlight.

He closed his eyes for a second and listened to the suffocating silence.

Chapter Nine

Pike shook off momentary despair and went to work. As kids they had once rigged a harness and lowered danger-loving Frankie into this pit. He'd reported that the ledge ate its way back into the earth, creating a sort of overhang about fifteen feet down. Pike uncoiled the rope from his shoulder and looped one end around an abandoned mining cart that was wedged against an outcropping of rocks. He quickly moved to the crevice and slipped over the side. Hand over hand, one foot wrapped around the rope, he made his way down until he landed a foot or so from Sierra's still form.

He took off his gloves and kneeled beside her, resting two fingers against her throat. The world realigned itself as her heartbeat leaped to his touch. He had no way of knowing if anything was broken. The inadequate light didn't reveal any obvious issues, but he wasn't sure.

As a precaution, he moved her a few more inches away from the edge, but he couldn't take her far as headroom tapered off quickly. Moving her revealed she'd been resting atop Tess's other pink shoe. Using the flashlight, he scanned for any sign of her.

Way back, deep under the overhang, a shape caught his eye. He stared at it until he was able to discern human features: dirt-matted hair, arms and legs all squeezed into a cranny. Tess had to have wiggled herself into this position, which meant she'd been alive after the fall. He got down on his stomach and dragged himself toward her. It was a tight fit and a huge relief when he was finally able to reach out and touch her arm. The light revealed cracked fingernails and rocks imbedded in her scratched hands.

"Tess," he called softly.

Her eyes fluttered open. He could barely see her features, but he could tell her expression went from frightened to relieved and back again in a single breath. "Pike!" she spluttered.

"What happened? Are you okay?"

"Are they gone?"

"Who?"

"Two guys. They…they threw me down here. They must have thought I went all the way to the bottom but my foot hit this ledge and I grabbed on. I don't know how I managed to climb up here. I just kept picturing that black hole…"

"They're gone," he assured her, though he had no way of knowing if they would come back or even if both of them had left. "Can you shift yourself so I can help get you out of there?"

"I'll try," she said.

A moment later, he was able to grasp her shoulders

and pull her farther toward the edge. Her coat was torn, her hair knotted. Her runny nose had smeared dirt across her cheeks. He handed her his bandanna. "Did all this happen when you fell?" he asked.

"Yeah," she said as she mopped her face. She looked down at her left foot and he directed the light. Her sock was torn and her foot was swollen. Tears appeared in her eyes. "It hurts."

He felt it gingerly, stopping when she cried out, but then her gaze traveled past him. "Sierra! Pike, when did she get here? What happened to her?"

"I was hoping you could tell me," he said.

She shook her head. "Where's Danny? Did they use me to trap him? I have to find Danny."

"Right now, we have to help Sierra," Pike said, scooting back to lift Sierra's hand and touch her face.

Tess crawled over to join him, dragging her injured foot. "Sierra, please, wake up."

To Pike's infinite relief, Sierra's eyes opened, but she blinked and furrowed her brow. He helped her roll over and sit. She moaned and clutched her head. He cradled her shoulders. "You're hurt," he said, feeling the top of her head and finding a noticeable bump. His hands ran down her arms, over her legs. "Does it hurt anywhere else?"

"It hurts everywhere," she whispered. "Pike, what happened?"

"You don't remember how you got down here?"

"No." She paused for a second. "No. I was looking for Tess." Her confused gaze switched to her sister. "Oh, my God, sweetheart, are you okay?"

"I don't know where Danny is!" Tess said as tears made more muddy tracks down her cheeks.

Pike and Sierra looked at each other, then Pike put an arm around Tess's shoulders. "We should have told you over the phone and then none of this would have happened. Danny is dead, honey. You were right, a man named Raoul Ruiz apparently killed him."

"How do you know? How can you be sure? What if—"

"We're sure," he said with just enough firmness to cut through her emotion. "We'll explain everything later. Right now we need to get you and Sierra off this ledge and out of this mine. You're both frozen and it's a long way home. Can I count on you?" Tess nodded.

The only place the ledge was open enough for a person to stand was right near the rim. He helped Tess first. She couldn't put weight on her foot and tumbled against him, but he managed to prop her against the rocks, where she held with a white-knuckled grip. Then he fashioned a loop in the end of the rope, tied a bowline knot and pulled it tight.

Now came the tough decision. How did he get both of these women up to the top? Did he leave the dazed one down here to wait her turn, hoping that she wouldn't fall over the edge? Or did he leave the one who couldn't even stand?

Sierra apparently sensed the dilemma. "Her first," she said through chattering teeth.

"Her first what?" Tess demanded.

"I have to go up to the top in order to pull each of you to safety," he said.

Tess clung to him a second. "Please don't leave us."

"I'm not leaving you. Wait for me to give you an all clear, then put the loop around your body and more or less sit on it. Use your good foot to keep yourself off the rock face. I'll pull you up."

He put his gloves back on, noticed Tess's other shoe nearby and grabbed it. It was for the injured foot so he tossed it aside. He turned his attention to Sierra. "Let me help you stand so you're ready when it's your turn." She leaned against him as he gently helped her to her feet. To his relief, she seemed pretty steady as she backed against the rock face beside Tess. He looked into her eyes a long moment and her lovely lips curved into a jittery smile.

"Cover your heads in case I knock dirt and rocks down as I go up," he said.

He hated leaving them twenty feet below, but there just wasn't any other way to get them out of here. He handed Sierra the good flashlight and took the weak one for himself. It didn't take light to get up to the mine floor on his own—it just took brawn.

Once he'd made it to the top, he took a couple of deep breaths. "Okay," he called, as he flicked on the weak light so he wouldn't trip and make a mess of things. He let the rope back down. "Make sure you hang on. You hear me, Tess?"

"I will," she called, but her voice sounded a hundred miles away.

He coiled the rope around the rock for extra leverage and began pulling to take up the slack. When he felt the rope tighten, he began the chore of hauling another person up a rock-and-dirt wall. For the first six feet, Tess was deadweight, but as she finally reached the side of the chasm, he felt the tension slacken as she apparently got her good leg under her and used her hands. Still, it was a great moment when he pulled her safely over the last of the edge, picked her up and carried her to the rock.

"Your turn," he called to Sierra.

Within minutes, he had grasped her under the arms and hauled her the last distance. Arm and arm, they staggered to the rock upon which Tess sat and, for a minute or two, hovered there in the ever diminishing glow of their one good flashlight.

"Look at my poor shoes," Sierra finally said as she straightened her legs to reveal her shredded black suede boots.

"They're done for," he said.

"They cost three hundred dollars."

He stuck out his foot to display tooled brown leather. "So did these."

"They look fine."

"Well, they're country boots. Yours are city boots."

"They used to be," she said. "Now they're garbage."

He picked up her hand and squeezed it and she smiled at him. The smile fled as she apparently heard an approaching noise at the same time he did. Tess whimpered and shrank against the rock. Someone was coming down the tunnel toward them. He put his finger against his lips and Sierra turned off her flashlight. Without that modest beam of light, the cavern seemed to close in around them, trapping them between the deep shafts and beyond the only exit. He picked up the shotgun.

The way he figured it, someone had meant for both women to disappear. The apparent roof collapse at the rim of the crevice indicated an accident. Without Tess's note, who knows when they would have looked for her here, but when they did, her abandoned shoe would suggest an explanation for her disappearance. Sierra's necklace would do the same for her. But why had the fake Danny asked Tess to wait for Sierra to accompany her? Was he aware that Sierra knew his identity? That had to be it.

And now? Had they come back to make sure the women had both died? Had they had second thoughts about the plausibility of their plot?

He hugged the wall and took a peek out into the main shaft. He could see lights, which made the people approaching pretty good targets. "Stop where you are!" he yelled.

"Pike!" a man responded.

"Gerard?"

Within seconds, all three of his brothers finally came into clear view. He'd never been happier to see them.

"You didn't text…"

"I forgot," he admitted.

"Did you find them? Are they okay?"

"More or less," he said.

"What can we do to help?" Gerard asked.

Frankie clapped Pike on the back. "Are you kidding? The professor here is the clever one in the family. I bet he's got this all figured out."

"Yeah," Pike said and grinned. "Sure I do."

SIERRA OPENED HER EYES. For a moment, she wasn't sure where she was or how she had gotten there. The room was dark, but that could be because of pulled shades. She sat up, which made her head ache, and looked around. Tess slept in the other twin bed. They were in the downstairs room Grace had insisted they use.

They were safe.

Now she remembered. Awakening on the ledge, Pike holding her, the impossibly long, cold ride home, Tess's grief, Grace's gentle care.

And more. She remembered more.

The door opened and Pike appeared. He smiled when he saw her and crossed the room. He hadn't shaved for over twenty-four hours and it looked as if he'd slept in his clothes. All in all, sexy as hell.

He sat down next to her. "How are you feeling?" he whispered.

She shrugged as she glanced at Tess. "How is she?"

"Grace thinks her ankle is sprained. She put a splint on it just in case something is broken. We can't get out of here yet because of the storm. You up to coming with me so we can talk?"

"Absolutely," she said and pulled down the sheets

to find that she was wearing her own nightclothes, which meant she wasn't wearing much.

"I guess I better put some clothes on," she said.

His lingering gaze and sudden wistful smile shot through her body. "Need any help?"

She leaned into him and touched his face with her own. His breath was warm against her chilled skin and he smelled like coffee and cinnamon. Delicious. She kissed his lips and for a second they just sat that way, content just to be together.

"Here," he whispered against her cheek and she pulled away to see that he held her diamond necklace. Her hand flew to her throat—she hadn't even noticed it was missing. "It was broken, but I fixed it," he said, and fastened it around her neck.

"Where did you find it?"

"In the mine. You have a red mark on the back of your neck. Someone must have ripped it off."

"My father gave me this," she said softly. "Thank you for fixing it."

He kissed her nose. "Up to rising now?"

"Yep." Various aches and pains announced themselves when she stood. They were explained by the bruises on her legs and arms. One knee hurt and her elbow was stiff. She found clean jeans in her suitcase, then pulled them over her hips and her green sweater over her head, wincing as the neckline tugged on her hair. Pike was suddenly there to smooth the sweater on its way and kiss her forehead.

"They hit my head before they threw me off the edge into the rift," she murmured.

He clasped her shoulders. "Do you remember what happened?"

"Bits and pieces."

They quietly left the bedroom and entered the empty kitchen. The view outside was blinding white—obviously it was still snowing.

"Is it a terrible storm?" she asked as she drew herself a glass of water.

"We've had worse. This one seems to be winding down already." He patted the stool. "Sit down, tell me what you remember."

She sat down across the island from him. "I remember seeing Tess's shoe on the ledge. Then there was a noise and a bright light. I turned around in time to see a man in a ski mask. He grabbed your Glock from my hand, struck me in the head and said something as I staggered away."

"What did he say?"

"I don't know. It was hard to understand him because of the mask, but it's more than just that." She paused for a second, thinking.

"What is it?" he asked. "Do you remember something else?"

"I was just thinking about a dream I had right before I found out that Tess was missing. Someone in a football helmet pinned me to the ground and called me an idiot." She bit her lip. "I don't think it was a premonition or anything."

"What happened next?"

"It all happened in the blink of an eye. He lifted me off my feet. The next thing I knew, I landed like a ton of bricks. I thought for sure every bone in my body was broken, but I was able to roll farther under the overhang. My eyes felt like they were spinning off into the dark. Then I heard voices and I realized there were two men up there. I think they were arguing about making sure I was dead. And then it sort of slipped away until all of a sudden, you were there."

He took her hand and rubbed her knuckles with his thumb. "What happened last night when you went to help your father and brothers find the film crew?" she asked.

"They were where I thought they'd be. A gunshot had spooked their horses. A couple were injured, the producer worst of all."

"A shot!" she said. "Doesn't that seem kind of co-incidental considering what was going on a mile or so over in the mine?"

"It does to me."

"How injured was the producer? Isn't his name Gary?"

"Yeah. Between Tess, him and you, Grace had her hands full. You have a slight concussion, Gary tore his rotator cuff when he put his hands out to stop his fall and a couple of the others are a little banged up, too."

"Did they see anyone at all?"

"No. They're convinced that the ex-employee who attempted to sue them tried another sabotage."

"Why would someone like him target Tess? And how would he even know about her in the first place?"

"I don't know," he said. "Unless there's a snitch in the crew."

"You mean someone on the film crew could be in cahoots with the ex-employee?"

"Yeah. It's no secret what Tess saw happen in LA. Everyone in the house is talking about it. For instance, who knows what a snitch might have overheard Grace telling my father, or what Frankie might have said in passing."

"Oh, man, I never thought of that."

"There's nothing to be done right now but keep a watchful eye. Do you want some tea or something to eat?"

"Tea sounds good," she said. "Did you guys find anything else in the gold mine?"

"Not really. There were a few shoe tracks too large to belong to you or Tess. It looks to me like someone's intention was to make your falls look like an accident. There was a lot of fresh rubble strewn around as though there'd been a collapse. It might have worked if the two of you hadn't been lucky enough to hit that ledge."

Sierra shuddered.

"Chance and Frankie looked for some indication of the snowmobile that I heard when I first got there," he continued. "They found a few tracks and deduced it must have headed to the main road, so that's where they went. They found additional tracks and a spot where a heavy vehicle had gotten stuck in the snow and then dug out. There were no people or machinery left behind, but it seems pretty clear someone brought a snow vehicle onto ranch land and contacted Tess to facilitate an ambush."

"If Raoul isn't behind this, why pick on Tess?"

"Maybe she seemed like a weak link to the snitch," Pike said as he got up to microwave a couple of cups of hot water. He dug tea bags from a canister.

"Did you look at the text Tess thought Danny sent?"

"I couldn't because they stole her phone. She did notice it wasn't his usual number."

"Probably a burner."

"Yeah," he said, handing her the hot cup.

"Some of this doesn't make sense," she added and rubbed her forehead. "Things aren't logical but I can't think clearly enough to figure out what's wrong."

"I can't, either," he admitted. "I'm brain-dead."

"Have you had any sleep?" she asked.

He smiled down into her eyes. "Not much."

"Maybe we should go…take a nap. Together, you know?"

He leaned down and kissed her. "I would love nothing more," he whispered against her lips. "Unfortunately, I have to meet up with Gerard and Chance to feed the cattle."

"How do you accomplish that in this weather?"

"We grow and store hay during the summer for times like this when field grazing is inaccessible. Then we load the hay onto a trailer and pull it out into the fields with a tractor. One of us drives and the two who pulled the shortest sticks get to ride on the back with pitchforks and drop the hay to hungry, frost-bitten cows. It's kind of fun in its own weird way."

Her expression looked incredulous. "I have work to do anyway," she said at last. "I haven't heard from Savannah in a while."

"Let me get your laptop for you," he said. "I saw it by the fireplace." He dashed out of the kitchen and was back with the laptop within seconds.

"By the way, I called the local law," Pike said as he handed her the computer. "They said they'll send someone out to check the mine when the weather calms down."

"I'll call the LAPD," she volunteered as she hit the button to power on the laptop.

"Do you miss New York?" Pike asked.

She nodded. "It's my home. Have you ever been there?"

He shook his head.

"Will you come visit me?" she asked.

"Is that an invitation?"

"Absolutely. It'll be fun to show you around. Spring is lovely."

"I bet," he said. "We'll have to get through calving, then I'm all yours."

"And then there's summer," she added, staring up at him. "I admit it's humid, but who has to go outside?"

"Summer is a busy time on a ranch," he said. He put his hand on her shoulder and added, "But I'll make time."

"Good. And then you have to see fall in the city. There's a big election this year for mayor. It'll be wild."

"Fall," he said. "Autumn is beautiful here."

"I bet."

He curled a piece of her hair around his finger. "Did you inherit your dad's interest in politics?"

"Not really. The guy I'm voting for is Maxwell Jakes. He's practically a shoo-in, mostly because the other guy is a first-class sleazeball. My dad would have approved, though. He was a one-party kind of guy and Jakes is the right party."

The sound of clomping came from the direction of the back bedroom and they both turned their heads. Tess appeared, awkwardly wielding a pair of crutches.

"Hey, look at you," Sierra said. Bruised, cut, bandaged and pale, the poor kid looked like she'd been through a wringer. For the first time that morning, Sierra wondered how she looked after the previous night's ordeal. "You have crutches lying around?" Sierra asked, glancing up at Pike.

"Dad said it was cheaper than renting them every time one of us hurt something," he said. He looked at Tess and added, "How are you feeling?"

"Kind of empty inside," she said.

"I'm sorry I had to tell you about Danny like I did."

"It's not your fault. I'm the one who snuck away. I'm the one who put both you guys in danger, something even my dad pointed out. I need a tissue. My nose is running."

"When did you talk to your dad?" Sierra asked as Pike slid a box of tissues toward Tess.

"Before I went to sleep," Tess said, dabbing at her nose. "You were already dead to the world. Aunt Grace said Dad deserved to hear from me before he heard from the police, so I woke him up and told him everything that's been happening." She looked down at her hands. "He says he wants me to come home."

"Of course he does," Pike said. "Would you like a cup of tea?"

She shook her head. "No thanks."

"Honey, can you remember anything else about the men in the mine?" Sierra asked. "Maybe something about their voices, for instance?"

"They didn't talk to me."

Pike turned his gaze to Sierra. "Do you remember something?"

"I'm not sure," she replied. "I told you one of them spoke to me. I don't know what he said. I'm not sure what's bothering me about it."

"I thought I was safe here," Tess blurted out, hugging herself and looking around the cheery room and shuddering. "I'm not safe anywhere, am I?"

"Tess—"

"I don't want to go talk to the LA police."

"We know," Sierra said. "Maybe, because of your foot, they can send detectives here to interview you."

Tess looked around the room again. "I don't want to stay here but I don't want to go there. I don't want to see the man who killed Danny, not ever, ever again."

"What about your father?" Sierra asked gently.

"He doesn't *really* want me to come," Tess said.

"Tess, you're his daughter."

"I'm just someone who gets in his way," she scoffed.

"Don't worry about it right now," Pike advised. "Come sit down."

"No thanks. I'm going to go sit by the fire," she said and Pike opened the door for her to make her way through to the dining room.

"Should we have warned her about the film crew?" Sierra asked after she left. "Where are they anyway?"

"Out in the barn shooting pictures of the horses and interviewing Kinsey and Gerard. I don't see any reason to feed Tess's active imagination. I know I'm the one who brought up a snitch in their ranks, but it's hard to really believe."

"I guess."

He pulled her to her feet and looked into her eyes. "Don't worry about her," he said.

Sierra leaned her head against his chest. "Things are going to get worse for her before they get better," she said. "Even if the LAPD sends detectives here to interview her, sooner or later she's going to have to go back for a trial."

"I know," Pike murmured. "In the end, she's going to have to face Raoul Ruiz." He kissed her forehead and she tilted her head so their lips could connect. The kiss was long and smoldering, and Sierra kind of lost track of herself as she ran her fingers through his hair.

The swinging door behind them ended the kiss. Harry Hastings stood framed in the doorway. His eyebrows inched up his forehead as he gazed at them, then he walked to the refrigerator.

"Time to meet up with my brothers," Pike said against Sierra's cheek and he kissed her a last time. "Later, Dad." Sierra watched him leave until Harry cleared his throat and her gaze swiveled to him. He took a can of soda from the fridge.

"Can I get you anything?" he asked her before he closed the door.

"No thanks," She glanced down to find she couldn't get an internet connection. "Drat," she murmured.

"Is there a problem?" he asked.

"The wireless must be down. May I restart your modem?"

"Lily already tried that this morning, didn't work. It's gotta be the tower outside of Falls Bluff. It's not uncommon after a storm like this, should be fixed in a day or so."

With a sigh, she closed the computer top and drummed her fingers. It seemed like forever since she'd checked email or anything else.

"Things move a little slower here than what you're used to," Harry added, pausing by her side. She looked up at him, trying to find some resemblance to Pike. Maybe around the eyes and certainly in height, but otherwise, she thought Pike resembled Mona more than his dad.

"I've noticed that," she said.

He rapped his knuckles on the countertop. "Do you use Facebook and Twitter?" he asked.

"Yes. Do you?"

"Waste of time," he said.

"Not in my line of work. What people post about themselves can be pretty revealing. Saves me a lot of legwork sometimes."

He laughed. "I bet. A lot of it's malicious nonsense, though."

"But it helps keep me in touch when I'm away. I like to know what's going on at home when I travel."

"That's right," he said slowly. Though the expression on his face was friendly, there was a glint in his eyes as he added, "You come from a long ways away."

"Yes, I do," she said.

"Not just in miles, either, right?"

"What do you mean?"

"Attitudes," he said. "Expectations. The ability to find contentment. People are different in a big city than on a little chunk of countryside, where they're outnumbered by cattle a hundred to one."

"I've heard it said that people are all the same deep down," she said.

He looked her straight in the eye. "You are a smart, accomplished woman, Sierra Hyde, but if you believe that, you're also naive. Well, I'd better get back. Tess is waiting for me to teach her how to play poker."

Sierra narrowed her eyes as he left the kitchen. She wasn't positive but she was pretty sure he'd just tried to tell her something important.

Chapter Ten

It was a subdued gathering that met for a late dinner around the big dining room table. People were just plain exhausted, injured, preoccupied or a combination of all three. Even the normally jovial film crew ate the beef stew Grace and Lily had labored over in introspective silence.

Pike examined each of them as they ate and he was hard-pressed to see a man among them who would attempt murder. It was one thing to feel sympathy for a former coworker and help him create nuisances; it was another thing entirely to help plot the murders of two innocent people. Sierra had said something wasn't logical. She was right. But what was it?

Toward the end of the meal, Gerard cleared his throat. "Today we found out that Leo is qualified to conduct wedding ceremonies," he announced. "I asked Kinsey what she thought about getting married right away, you know, like tomorrow."

"And I said tomorrow would be great," Kinsey said.

Lily squealed. "That's fantastic!"

"Will you be my maid of honor?"

"Of course I will," Lily said.

"And Pike," Gerard said, "will you stand up with me?"

"You bet. Do you have a license and all that?"

"We arranged everything a month or so ago," Gerard said. "License, rings, the whole shebang. Leo being able to marry us made the timing perfect."

"I got ordained online so I could marry my cousin and her husband last year," Leo explained. "Doing this sure beats the heck out of watching it snow."

"And it will be fun to have the wedding before Sierra has to leave," Kinsey added.

"That would be nice," Sierra said with a quick glance at Pike.

"This is wonderful news," Grace declared with moist eyes. "Let's have the ceremony in the evening, okay, so I have time to get things ready."

"Perfect," Kinsey said. "Thanks."

"I'm the one who should be thanking you," Grace said softly. "All those years ago I named you Sandra and when you came back into my life, you were Kinsey. At first I was sad you kept that name and then I realized it didn't matter—what mattered was *who* you were and that we had a chance to get to know each other again." Her eyes suddenly grew wide. "But Kinsey, your grandmother won't be here for your wedding. We both owe her so much."

"Not to worry," Kinsey said. "I spoke to her this afternoon. She urged me to go ahead. We'll fly to

New Orleans when the baby comes. That's all she really cares about."

"Then it's perfect," Grace said. "Oh, Harry, there's going to be a wedding on the ranch and then a baby! And it's all happening tomorrow!"

"Not all of it, at least not tomorrow," Kinsey said, patting her stomach.

"I couldn't be happier for you both," Pike's dad said. His gaze shifted to Sierra and he smiled at her. She glanced down at her plate and pushed a piece of carrot around with a fork.

Then the old man turned his attention to Charlie and patted his knee. "Come here, boy," he said and Charlie gleefully joined the man he considered his grandfather. Pike glanced at Chance and Lily as they watched this sweet little scene unfold and he knew a second wedding wasn't far off.

Did he ever think about marrying? Maybe in a vague, someday sort of way, at least until recently. He glanced at Sierra. She was still pursuing the carrot with her fork and didn't meet his gaze.

They all pitched in and cleared the table and did the dishes before they began wandering off to read or go to bed. Though the electricity was on and the television worked, the satellite receiver wasn't functioning, no doubt due to how much snow had accumulated in the dish. Not that he minded. Snowed-in days were good times to draw close, to talk to others in the family and reconnect. He was looking forward to taking Sierra home to his barn, and he found her in the back bedroom with Tess. The two sisters were sitting side by side on one of the twin beds, Sierra's arm around Tess's shoulder. Tess's eyes were blood-shot and her cheeks tear-streaked.

He sat down on Tess's other side to lend support. Eventually, Tess excused herself to go wash her face and that left him and Sierra sitting alone.

"All the talk about a wedding got to her," Sierra said. "She's built Danny into the love of her life. I think I'd better stick close to her tonight."

Disappointment flared, but he knew she was right. "Yeah, I can see that. Did you get a hold of Detective Hatch this afternoon?"

"Yes. He was shocked that Raoul Ruiz might have traveled here to silence Tess."

"It seems strange to me, too," Pike said.

"Yeah. Well, Hatch assured me that Tess doesn't have to fly back to LA for questioning yet. They'll send detectives to interview her here or even in New York if she decides to come home with me."

He stared at her a second as though surprised. "Have you decided when you're leaving?"

"As soon as I can," she said. "I have obligations… You know how it is. I haven't talked to Tess yet about coming with me."

"This seems sudden," he said softly.

She studied her hands for a second before darting him a quick glance. "Did you notice the way your father looked at me?"

"He likes you," Pike said.

She shot him another look. "I don't know if he

does or not, but I do know he doesn't think I'm good enough for you."

"That's crazy. If anything he thinks you're way out of my league."

"I don't mean not good enough in the sense that I'm not smart enough or something. Earlier today, he started talking about New York… It sounded like he was reminding me that you and I are from two different worlds."

"So what?" he said. "There's nothing wrong with that."

"It got me thinking," she continued, still avoiding his gaze. "I don't fit in here. I'm not the kind of woman your father wants for you."

He took both her hands in his. "Sierra, even if that were true, and I'm not saying it is, I'm not a kid. My father doesn't get to decide who I care about or spend my time with."

"But the thing is, I see his point."

"We talked about our relationship right from the start," he said. "There were ground rules. I haven't meant to cross them—"

"It's not you," she interrupted. "It's me."

"What are you talking about?"

"We were supposed to keep this thing between us light and breezy and then today I invited you to New York to experience every little season. Why did I do that?"

"Why?" he repeated. "Because we like each other? Because we want to spend time together?"

"No, Pike. The real reason is deeper and more

self-serving. I think I wanted to see how you fit into my world. I can't imagine living here, but I don't think you can live any other way. These people... I don't even know what I'm doing here."

"You're helping Tess—"

"Am I? What exactly have I done for her?"

He squeezed her hands. "*We* are both trying to keep her alive. *That's* the major reason you are here." He lifted her chin with his fingers and lowered his voice. "Don't jump so far ahead when it comes to us. I promised you I could handle things and I will. No one has to move anywhere or live a life they don't want."

"Ah, Pike, all the good intentions in the world don't mean a thing when your heart gets involved. You know that."

His brow furrowed. "What exactly are you trying to say?"

She closed the gap between them and touched her lips to his. His hopes swelled and then shrank as she whispered, "I need to step back."

"From me?"

"Yes."

"Is everything okay?" a voice asked from the doorway, and they both turned to see Tess standing there. She hobbled over to them using one crutch and the furniture for support. She looked from one of them to the other. "What's wrong with you guys?"

"We're just tired," Sierra said. "Everybody in this house is just flat-out exhausted."

Pike knew it was time to leave. He stood up, ruffled Tess's hair and walked to the door. "See you guys tomorrow," he said, his gut clenching at the look in Sierra's eyes. Her gaze dropped to her hands and he closed the door.

What had just happened?

He ran into Chance in the mudroom, where his brother was pulling on rubber boots. "Man, I hate going back to my place all alone," Chance said. "Lily wants to wait to get married until this fall but I don't think I'm going to make it that long. I want her and Charlie at my place with me."

Pike sat down beside his brother. "Let me ask you a question," he said.

"Sure."

"You used to play the field."

Chance nodded. "Yep."

"I think I need some pointers on how to do it."

Chance laughed. "Isn't it too late for that?"

"What do you mean too late?"

"I just got the impression that you and Sierra had something special going on."

"I've known her less than a week," Pike said.

Chance smiled. "I remember the first time I saw Lily. That was it for me, but everyone around here, including you, recognized it before I did."

"It's not like that with me and Sierra," Pike said.

"Yeah." Chance clapped him on the back, added a good-night and went out the back door into the cold, snowy world. Pike followed a few minutes later, and not long after that pulled up in front of his barn on the snowmobile. The headlight illuminated Daisy, who had heard the engine and had come outside to wag a greeting.

He trudged through the snow and kneeled down to pat her and she followed him inside. Once in the kitchen, he poured kibble into her bowl and the cat's, refilled water dishes and grabbed himself a beer.

He sat down on the sofa and looked around the huge space. He'd never really thought too much about it, but in the back of his mind he knew he'd built this place for a future family. There should be kids in the loft rooms giggling themselves to sleep, a woman by his side who shared his values and hopes.

He heard Sierra's voice in his head. She said his family didn't approve of her. What if the truth was that she didn't approve of them?

A streak of black announced Sinbad's presence as he jumped onto the back of the sofa and curled his tail around his own feet. Daisy's toenails clicked against the wood floors as she crossed the room to join them. It took her a few seconds to haul her pregnant body up onto the couch beside him, where she turned around twice before settling with her head in his lap. He smoothed her soft ears and she looked up at him with huge brown eyes.

He'd done the dumbest thing in the world when it came to securing happiness. He'd fallen for a woman who'd warned him a relationship with her would be "terminal." She'd known the minute she stepped foot on this ranch that she would never dream of staying. She'd been open and honest about it. He'd been the delusional one.

"Well, you guys," he said, looking at his critters. "Looks like it's you and me."

SIERRA WOKE UP to find Tess's bed was empty. She looked out the big window that faced the icy river and found the sun shining. The glare from the snow was amazing. City snow wasn't quite this white and pure. Ordinarily, such beauty coming on the heels of the last two days would have lifted her spirits, but today it was going to take more than a change in the weather.

For a second she lay there. This room was close to the kitchen and she could smell the aroma of a baking cake—Kinsey and Gerard would be married this evening and apparently Grace was getting an early start.

Had she really broken things off with Pike last night? Silly question—she knew she had. And she also knew he would not push or cajole her into re-thinking her decision. For better or worse, the deed was done.

And yet the thought that he wasn't hers anymore to touch or kiss was hard to swallow and impossible not to regret. She got out of bed, washed up and brushed her teeth, gathered her hair in a ponytail and put on the green sweater. Her first priority of the day was to make sure Tess was safe and then make arrangements to fly home using the open-ended ticket Pike had purchased when she came here days before.

The smell of cake was too sweet for so early in the day. She comforted herself by thinking of the

deli down the block from her apartment. The day
after tomorrow, she'd feast on bagels and lox and
drink coffee so strong it had the power to kick-start
the lousiest day. She'd have to settle for toast this
morning, though she couldn't fault the ranch coffee.
It was as strong as the stuff she bought. But how did
these people survive the afternoon without a cappuc-
cino or espresso?

Tess was seated at the counter eating cereal and
doodling on some paper as Grace took the first of
three round cake pans from the oven. "Sleep well?"
she asked as she set each on a rack.

"Yes, thanks," Sierra said.

"Liar," Tess said. "You tossed and turned all night."

Sierra sat across from her sister. "I was having
dreams."

"About falling?" Tess asked, her eyes suddenly
fearful.

"No. I dreamed a bald guy was poking a stick at
me through a window blind. I tried to stop him and
he bit me. Stupid stuff that just made me restless."
She looked at the paper upon which Tess had doo-
dled. "What are you doing?"

"Grace said I could decorate Kinsey's cake. I was
thinking of flowers with little silver balls in the center. Or we could bake sugar cookie hearts and frost
them and then stick them on the cake. I saw it in a
magazine and it was cool."

"You have an artistic streak so whatever you decide will be perfect. Listen, honey, we need to talk
about what you want to do on a long-term basis,"

she added. "It's time for me to go home and get back to work."

"You're leaving?" Tess asked.

"I have a job to get back to. I was thinking you could come with me."

"To New York? I don't know."

At the sink, Grace leaned forward to peer out the window. "Who's that?" she murmured. She turned to look back at Sierra. "A car just pulled in. I know Harry got up early and plowed the ranch road, but I didn't know the roads from town were clear."

"Maybe a neighbor," Tess said.

Grace looked out the window again. "I don't recognize the car."

Tess craned her neck to look, but Sierra touched her sister's hand to reclaim her attention. "I want to book a flight as soon as possible. If you want to come with me, I need to get you a ticket."

"I don't know," Tess said.

"The other option is you stay here with Pike," Sierra added.

"I guess I should talk to him."

"That's a good idea."

"The man getting out of the car looks vaguely familiar," Grace said as she continued staring.

"Maybe he's with the local police," Sierra offered. "Pike said they would come out here to investigate when the weather cleared."

"It's not a police car and the man isn't dressed like an officer. In fact, his clothes are all wrong."

Sierra popped to her feet. All she could think was

that it must be trouble. A knock sounded on the door. She fought the urge to grab a butcher knife and went to open it.

For a second she just stared at the familiar features, almost unable to reconcile this man's presence on the Hastings Ridge Ranch. He was dressed in pressed jeans and alligator loafers—no socks. His concession to the cold seemed to be a blazer and his graying blond hair was slicked back from his tanned face. "Doug?"

"I thought I'd never find this godforsaken place!" he said under his breath. "It's freezing out here. How do people live like this?"

"Does Tess know you're coming?"

"No, I wanted to surprise her."

"Dad!" Tess squealed from the kitchen, obviously recognizing his voice. "Is that really you?"

Doug smiled broadly, his dimples all but twinkling as he stamped the snow off his loafers and sidled past Sierra. "Do I hear my girl?" he called as he strode through the mudroom.

Sierra closed the door. In the kitchen, she found Doug kneeling in front of his daughter, examining her foot without touching it. He looked like a handsome doctor on a soap opera. "Does it hurt?" he asked. "Has it been X-rayed?"

"We've been snowed in. It really hurts, though."

"It appears to be a bad sprain to me," Grace said from the sink. "I wrapped and iced it but now that the roads are clear and you're here, maybe you could drive her into Falls Bluff to the urgent care center."

"Of course I will," he said as he stood.

Sierra realized Doug and Grace had never met and performed introductions. "I remember your TV show," Grace said. "I was a big fan."

"Thank you," he said graciously.

"Are you doing anything right now besides those clever insurance ads?"

"I have my fingers in a few things," he said, then hitched his hands on his waist and looked around the kitchen. "This is such a cozy cabin. And that cake smells delightful."

"It's a wedding cake," Tess said. "Gerard and Kinsey are getting married tonight." She showed him her doodling and added, "I'm going to decorate it."

"Very cute," he said and turned back to Grace. "How do I wangle an invitation to this wedding?"

She laughed. "We'd love to have you. In fact, where are you staying while you're here?"

"I'll get a room in town—"

"Nonsense, you're Tess's father. There's plenty of room here."

This rambling house was no more a "cozy cabin" than a cruise ship was a rowboat, but saying there was plenty of room right now was something of a stretch. With four people in the film crew, her and Tess and now Doug, even this big house was popping at the seams.

"Why are you in Idaho?" Sierra asked, alarmed at how chilly her voice sounded. Her experience with this man had led her to believe he did very little that wasn't self-serving, but there was no reason to be rude to him, especially when she knew her current bad mood had more to do with herself than with him.

"How could I not come when I heard how distraught Tess was? A girl needs her father after an ordeal like the one she suffered, right, honey?"

Tess smiled and Sierra began a slow thaw toward the man. Maybe he'd come to his senses and realized the very real danger still looming over Tess. For her sake, Sierra sure hoped so.

Doug looked toward the swinging door. "I heard there was a film crew here," he said.

"The movie people are setting up for the wedding out in the barn," Grace said. "All except for Gary, the producer, who's still in bed because he tore his rotator cuff and he's having trouble sleeping."

Doug nodded. "You mean Gary Dodge. Fine man."

"Are you friends?"

"Never met him, but I pride myself on thorough research. So the others are outside, huh? Maybe I'll go shoot the breeze with them."

"But what about my foot?" Tess asked. "I think I should get an X-ray now so I'll have time to decorate the cake when we get back."

"Sure, sure," he said. "We will, but there's no rush, is there?"

"Well, there kind of is because of the cake and everything. I was hoping we could talk about things."

"Lots of time for that." He tousled the top of his daughter's head, smiled at Grace, avoided Sierra's gaze and left the house.

Grace's gaze shifted to Sierra. Sierra glanced at

Tess, who had turned on the stool to watch her father's retreat. Her furrowed brows and down-turned mouth made her appear older and more jaded than she had just a few minutes before. Longing to see Tess smile, Sierra trotted out her cheeriest voice. "Have you decided how you're going to decorate this cake?"

"No," Tess said.

Sierra bit her lip and brought her voice down a bit. "Listen. I know you want to catch up with your dad, but I'd be happy to drive you into Falls Bluff to have your foot X-rayed and you guys can visit later."

"No thanks," she said listlessly.

"I thought your foot was killing you."

She shrugged.

"Hmm. Well, I wanted to tell you that if you decide to come to New York with me, we'll turn my office into your bedroom. You can paint it any color you want. And there are lots of colleges and programs—"

"Just stop!" Tess interrupted, anger flashing in her eyes. "Don't worry about me, okay? I can take care of myself. I don't need anyone else." She grabbed her crutches and hobbled back to the bedroom, slamming the door behind her.

Sierra looked after her sister with wide eyes.

Grace squeezed her hand. "Give her time, dear. It's not your love and acceptance that she's looking for."

AFTER RETRIEVING HER COMPUTER, Sierra made her way to the room with the fireplace, glad to find it empty. She desperately wanted to book a flight home. Until

Tess made up her mind about her future, that wasn't going to happen.

Being stuck inside this house, where everything reminded her of Pike, was difficult. Part of her waited with bated breath for him to walk into a room and the other part of her dreaded the moment she'd look into his eyes. She knew she'd hurt him and even if it kept him from deeper hurt ahead, it felt lousy.

No use thinking about that now. Instead she was relieved to find that the internet was working again, and she focused her attention on wading through emails, none of which were from Savannah.

Wasn't that kind of strange?

Next she accessed a news website to catch up on what was happening at home. The garbage company was threatening a strike and two Yankees were accused of wife-swapping, but the big story had to do with the murder of a call girl named Giselle Montgomery and the burgeoning scandal involving evidence that she had been linked to one of the mayoral candidates. No surprise that it was the sleazeball candidate, Ralph Yardley. Sierra mentally patted herself on the back for supporting Jakes. No one had accused Yardley of the actual murder, as he had an ironclad alibi involving a fund-raising dinner he attended with his wife. The innuendo was that he could have hired someone to take care of Giselle if she had threatened to reveal an affair.

The poor woman had drowned and her body had been found in the Hudson River. There was evidence she had been dumped, the report stated without going into details.

There was also a tantalizing sidebar piece that linked the murdered call girl to the notorious Broadway Madame, who was only notorious because nobody knew exactly who she was. Sierra thought for a moment about the difference between her city's news and the news out of Falls Bluff. New York City may have a seedy underbelly, but it was here in the country that she'd been thrown down a chasm and left for dead.

She took care of a few loose ends with clients, made a lunch date for later in the week with a couple of girlfriends and wrote Savannah an email asking if everything was okay. She didn't look up until Gary entered the room. He held his arm kind of funny due to his injury. "Morning," he said, looking around. "Where is everybody?"

"Grace said your crew is out setting up for the wedding in the barn."

"In the barn?" He looked surprised. "It's cold out there. Why don't they have the ceremony in this beautiful room?"

"I don't have the slightest idea," Sierra said. "Gary, there's something else. The police will be here pretty soon now that the roads are clear. They have to be told about your old employee on the off chance he's somehow behind what happened. If you don't tell them, I'm afraid I'll have to."

"I'll talk to them," he said. "Damn."

"Sorry."

"Can't be helped. Nothing good ever comes from trying to ignore reality, does it?"

"No," she said softly. "Not really."

A few seconds later, Doug waltzed into the den and did a double take when he saw Gary. He held out his hand and strode over to him. Gary looked nervous for a moment as though afraid Doug would jar his arm, but Doug seemed to recall the injury and dropped his hand. "Just the man I wanted to see," Doug said. "I've heard good things about the quality of your projects, Gary."

"Thank you. Have we met?"

"No, I don't believe so. I've heard of you, though. My name is Douglas Foster."

"That's why you look familiar. You were in that detective show years ago. What are you up to now?"

"I'm the voice for Safer Insurance Company. Maybe you've heard my ads."

"Sure, yeah." Gary narrowed his eyes. "They're excellent." He chewed on his bottom lip and added, "How coincidental that you're here."

"Not entirely," Sierra said. "Doug is Tess's father. He came when he heard what happened to her at the mine."

"Poor kid was really roughed up," Gary said. His gaze shifted to Sierra and she got the feeling he was willing her not to mention his disgruntled former employee and the possibility he'd been behind almost killing Doug's daughter. Probably worried about attorneys and more lawsuits. She had no intention of saying anything so she produced a reassuring smile.

Doug nodded. "Yeah, she sounded terrible on the phone. I just had to come and offer support. But it's great that you're here. I'm fascinated by your project concerning this ranch and its lurid past."

Gary stared at Doug for a few moments, assessing him, apparently, because Sierra saw in his eyes the moment he reached a decision. "It might be even better luck than you think," Gary said. "Unforeseen circumstances with our voice-over talent have left us without a narrator."

"Nothing serious, I hope."

"Actually yes, he had a stroke."

"Oh, you're talking about Patrick Nestle. Great guy. I heard about the stroke."

"His withdrawal has left us in a little bit of a bind. I need to check with my crew right now. Do you have time this afternoon to talk or would you prefer your agent be present?"

"No need for my agent at this point," Doug said. "Sure, I have the rest of this day. Just let me know when you want to sit down for a while."

"I don't want to get in the way of you and your daughter—"

Doug interrupted him with a laugh. "Tess? Oh, she'll understand. There's always tomorrow."

"Good." They exchanged business cards, Sierra supposed so they'd have each other's cell phone numbers, and Gary left to find breakfast. Doug shoved his hands in his designer-jean pockets, rocked back on his heels and smiled.

"You know, I don't think I really believed it till

just now," Sierra said, closing the laptop and shaking her head as she stood.

"Believed what?"

"You. Why you're here."

"I'm here for Tess."

"Like hell you are. You're here for you. You're here on a job interview. Tess was simply your ticket in the door. And the worst part is that she knows it. You almost had me fooled, but she saw right through you."

"You don't know what you're talking about," he scoffed and started to turn.

"Don't walk away just yet," Sierra said, and he paused. "You and I have never been friendly and that's okay. I don't need you or your reputation or your money. But Tess does. For better or worse, she is your kid and she loves you."

"Is that why she ran away with that druggie and didn't bother calling?" he said with a sneer.

"You know, it just may be. Danny was quite a bit older than her. Maybe she was looking for a father figure."

"That's a bunch of mumbo jumbo."

"Doug, please," Sierra said, lowering her voice and reining in her frustration. "Tess witnessed the cold-blooded murder of somebody she cared about. Whether or not the murderer was behind what happened here in the mine, she has to go back to Los Angeles and finger the man she saw kill Danny. After that, she'll be the star witness at his trial and because she's your daughter and you possess a certain amount of fame, she'll be under scrutiny. She's going to have to cope with all of this. I have offered to help her, so has Pike, but in her heart of hearts, she wants you."

"No, she doesn't," he said and damn if he didn't look as though he actually believed it.

"Sierra is right," Tess said from the doorway, where she balanced on the crutches. Her face was blotchy, her eyes red. Sierra knew that the incident in the mine had terrified Tess even more than she'd let on and that dealing with the growing fear of another attempt wore on her mind. Sometimes she could shrug it off and pretend things were okay, but now and again, things just snapped.

And then her dad had come and a leap of hope for his support had been dashed on the sharp edges of his ego.

"Tess," he said.

"I thought you came here because you loved me but you really came for a job, didn't you?"

"You're just saying that because Sierra said it."

She shook her head. "No, I'm not. I knew it the minute you couldn't wait to ditch me so you could hang out with the film crew." Her lips quivered. "It's not like you haven't done the same thing a hundred times before."

"Tess, you're exaggerating—"

"Am I? A crazy, drugged-out lunatic tried to kill me. I bet you wish he'd succeeded. Then I'd be out of your hair forever. I wish I would have died with Danny!"

"Tess!" Doug said, his eyes almost spinning. "Don't talk like that, please, honey."

"It's the truth," she sobbed. "I wish I were dead."

Her declaration practically ignited the air in the room. Doug's expression turned even more bewildered and when he finally spoke, his voice sounded shaken. "Oh, Lord, what have I done? How do I fix this? Tell me what you want."

"I want you to love me," she whispered.

Sierra took a step toward comforting her, but Doug held up his hands and shook his head. It was he who walked to Tess's side and draped an arm around her shoulders. "I've always loved you, baby," he said as he helped her to the sofa, where the two sat down. Tess's trembling hands worried the bottom hem of her sweater as Doug continued talking softly to her. "Sometimes I'm a tad selfish, I know that. But hurting you…well, that was never my goal. If you want, I'll help you face whatever lies ahead."

"I don't know how you can," she said.

"Listen. Mona and I split up, this time for good. I'll rent us an apartment with great security. We'll get to know each other again. Trust me just this one more time. Give me another chance, please, Tess."

She stared at him for several seconds and then nodded.

"Good. We'll leave right now if you want."

"What about Gary and the documentary?"

"Gary will understand. We can meet later if he's

still interested. As of right now, you are the main priority."

"Then I'd like to wait until after the wedding," Tess said. She looked up at Sierra. "Are you okay with this?"

"Absolutely. I'll give you the contact information for the detective we talked to at the LAPD. All I want is for you to be safe and happy, Tess."

"We'll drive in for that X-ray now," Doug said.

An unexpected tap on Sierra's shoulder surprised her and she whirled around. Two hands caught her arms and steadied her. She looked up into Pike's eyes and a jolt of pain shot through her chest. It was obvious to her that he'd rather be anywhere on earth than standing next to her.

"We need to talk," he said as he lowered his hands and backed away.

She followed him from the room.

Chapter Eleven

Despite the dark circles under her eyes, Sierra looked as gorgeous as ever to Pike. Her creamy skin glowed, begging him to extend a hand and touch her. Instead he spoke. "Robert is here to talk to you. He's waiting in the kitchen. He's also sent a crew out to the gold mine."

She blinked. "Who is Robert?"

"Sorry. Officer Robert Hendricks. He's an old friend."

They were standing in the foyer and Sierra glanced back at the sofa at Tess. "Does he want to see us both at the same time?" she asked.

"No. He said you go in first and then Tess. When did Doug show up?"

She lowered her voice. "A couple of hours ago. Tess must have told him about the documentary, probably including the fact that they'd lost their actor for the voice-overs. He came to try to finagle a job out of Gary, but Tess just convinced him to take her back to LA."

Pike's brow furrowed. "What? I thought she was adamant about not going back there."

"So did I. I'm beginning to think the past three or four months have been a cry for his attention. Maybe he'll finally understand she needs some guidance."

Pike rubbed his forehead. "You're going to have to give me a minute or two to wrap my head around Doug providing guidance."

She touched his hand. "Pike, I want to tell you that I'm sorry about last night. I regret, well, things."

He looked down at her, desire pulsing through his veins like acid. "What exactly do you regret?" he asked.

"We'd all had such a lousy couple of days. I wish I hadn't dumped that on you, too."

"So you don't regret walking away from me exactly, just the way you did it?"

She nodded.

"Water under the bridge," he said. "Have you made plans to return home?"

"Not yet. I was waiting for Tess to decide what she wanted. Now that it appears Doug is back in the picture I'll make arrangements."

They stared at each other. He could not bring himself to break the connection until she raised her hand and touched his cheek so gently it stopped his heart. He nodded once, opened the front door and left.

AS BEST MAN, Pike dressed in his good suit, a tailored black ensemble with a longer-than-average jacket and country tailoring at the shoulders. He didn't wear it very often; in fact, he found a folded wedding invitation to Gerard's first wedding in the pocket. The joy of that day had been eclipsed a few years later by a tragic accident. Pike tossed the embossed paper into the fireplace before he fed Daisy, made sure she was comfortable and took off for the main ranch house. The dog had been acting squirrelly that day. He had a feeling motherhood was impending and he hated leaving her alone.

On the other hand, he wouldn't miss seeing Gerard and Kinsey tie the knot for the world.

He found the outside of the barn illuminated with tiny white lights, and when he walked inside, he realized he was the only one there. For a second, he stood inside the door and gazed around at what the film crew had done to ready the space for a country wedding.

Lanterns hung on every post, casting warm yellow light. A few parabolic heaters kept the space warm. Bales of hay had been lined up in rows to act as seats for the guests, while wedding bells consisted of his dad's collection of old cowbells strung together on ropes. A makeshift arch had been draped with evergreen boughs and a lopsided but charming cake, decorated with what appeared to be cookies, sat amid a small sea of twinkling champagne flutes on a trestle table covered with a gingham cloth.

He sat down on a hay bale and folded his hands between his knees. His eyes closed for a moment, but he found no relief from his ping-ponging feelings. As happy as he was that Gerard had found love a second time, he couldn't help but wonder if he would ever find it even once.

A voice came from behind him. "What do you think? Looks pretty good, doesn't it?"

Pike jumped to his feet and turned to find Ogden and Leo walking into the barn. Ogden carried a guitar. "Yeah, you guys did great," Pike said.

"Going to be a nice wedding," Leo said. "We took the precaution of locking the dogs in another outbuilding. Frankie said we couldn't trust them with the cake."

"Good thinking," Pike said.

Over the course of the next thirty minutes, members of the household filtered into the barn while Ogden played the guitar and Oliver filmed the arrivals. Chance and Charlie stood with Pike for a while before sitting down. Doug made his trademark big entrance, but not alone this time. Instead, he carried Tess to a bale of hay, where he helped her sit. There was a blue walking cast on her foot now, but what was really different was the smile on her face. For the first time in a long time, his little sister actually looked happy. As did Grace and Harry, who arrived holding hands.

Sierra showed up at last wearing a slim skirt and an ivory-colored scoop-necked sweater. He recognized Grace's green cashmere shawl draped over her shoulders. She looked stunning.

"This is lovely," she said as she paused in front of him. Her hair was gathered at the nape of her neck, but glistening tendrils fell against her cheeks. Her sparkling eyes gave the diamond pendant a run for its money.

"Beautiful," he said as he stared at her.

"I talked to Detective Hatch this afternoon. He had big news. I haven't shared it with Tess yet. May we talk after the wedding?"

"Sure," he said.

Frankie and Gary ushered in Gerard at last. Gary was still protecting his shoulder and chose a bale of hay near the back on which to perch. Frankie found a seat next to Chance and Charlie as Pike and Gerard walked to the arch.

"You ready for this?" Pike asked his big brother.

Gerard's blue eyes danced. "I can't wait."

Holding a modest bouquet and dressed in rose, Lily entered next and slowly moved up the makeshift aisle. Oliver changed position to catch everything with the camera. Ogden played the guitar until Lily stopped to stand beside Pike. Then he began strumming the familiar tune of the wedding march.

All eyes turned to witness Kinsey float into the barn, a vision in white. As pretty as the dress was, it was the way she looked at Gerard that fascinated Pike. He glanced at his brother and saw the same look of anticipation. His gaze moved to Sierra, whose head was still turned.

Leo began the ceremony and Kinsey and Gerard didn't take their eyes off each other's faces until they finally exchanged vows, rings and kisses and Leo pronounced them husband and wife.

Again, Pike's gaze strayed to Sierra and this time he found her looking straight at him.

"RAOUL RUIZ IS DEAD?" Pike said a little later as he and Sierra stood off to the side, their heads bent in conversation.

He was so close she could smell his aftershave, a scent she hadn't realized until that moment had earned a spot in her subconscious. "He apparently overdosed," she said. "Detective Hatch says he's been dead at least four days, maybe more. They found his body in Tess's blue car parked in a remote way station out in the desert. The speculation is that he decided to take off for parts unknown after he killed Dwayne."

"Then he couldn't have been in Idaho when you and Tess were attacked," Pike said.

"Nope. And they found his phone on his body. He hadn't sent any texts to Tess. It doesn't appear he had a thing to do with the mine."

"Did you tell Officer Hendricks?"

"I called him. He'd already talked to the LAPD. He said the techs found a few interesting things in the mine, including a gas lantern and a matchbook that was apparently used to light it."

"Did they find fingerprints on the lantern?"

"None. He thinks they must have worn gloves, which makes sense considering how cold it was."

"What about the matchbook?"

"It's for a bar called The Pastime. Why does that sound familiar?"

"We parked across the street from it the day we took Tess in after her overdose," Pike said. "It's a local hangout."

"I didn't realize I had even noticed it. Well, the matchbook was apparently ground into the dirt and damaged. The lab is looking at it."

"And that's it?"

"Besides footprints and things like that, pretty much. He said he'd be in touch."

Pike nodded but looked distracted. "I guess the million-dollar question, now that Raoul has been eliminated as a suspect, is who else wants you and Tess dead."

"Me? Oh, no. I was an afterthought."

"Were you? You're forgetting how spooked you were when you arrived on this ranch. You were looking over your shoulder, remember?"

"I kind of forgot about that," she said. "But that has nothing to do with here. That started on the last night I worked back east."

"Maybe that's where it started. A couple of things have bothered me all along. Why did they ask Tess to bring you with her? And why not just shoot you? If the purpose was murder—they had guns—why risk throwing you in a pit?"

"Good questions. But maybe those facts fit with it being the old LOGO employee. In that case, the intent wasn't murder, just sabotage."

"How would someone like that get Tess's number?" Pike protested. "How did he know to call himself Danny? How in the world did he find the mine in that weather?"

"Tess could have told him, or he could have looked it up. Information is easier to get than it used to be, you know."

He shook his head.

"And one of the crew could be involved," she said.

"I can't believe that. I know, I know, I'm the one who suggested it, but it just doesn't make sense. There were two men in the mine and the entire crew has an alibi for that time period—they were all out with us at the hanging tree. So now you have a snitch, a crazy ex-employee and someone else all in on a reckless act of sabotage?"

"It looks like it," Sierra said.

"I don't buy it. Anyway, I mentioned all this to Officer Hendricks and he said he would contact Seattle police and see if anyone has a record. Have you remembered anything else about the attack? Have you figured out what they said that bugged you?"

"No. But I had another dream about a bald guy."

He raised his eyebrows. "What?"

She'd apparently never mentioned her recent nocturnal preoccupation with hairless men. "Never mind," she said.

"Did you book a flight to New York?"

"I'm on standby."

"You'll need a ride to the airport."

"Doug and Tess are flying out very early tomorrow. I'll ride to the airport with them."

"When are you going to tell Tess about Raoul?"

"In the morning, during the drive. No need for her to lay awake all night trying to figure things out."

For several heartbeats they stared at each other.

This was it. They'd caught up with the news. There was no more to say; it was time to walk away and not look back.

Pike took the first step. "Then this is goodbye."

She swallowed. "I guess so."

He touched her hair and kissed her forehead. "Have a good life," he whispered, then turned and walked over to join his brothers. Sierra told herself she was exhausted and went to bed.

SOMETIME AROUND MIDNIGHT, she gave up trying to sleep. Not knowing who would be up and wandering around the house, she dressed in jeans and a sweater, grabbed what she needed and quietly exited the room so as not to wake Tess. Parking herself on a stool in front of the counter, she opened her laptop and typed *breaking news* into the search engine.

This time, the philandering baseball players had been kicked off page one and replaced by a trio of photographs. One was of the murdered call girl, the next was Ralph Yardley and the last was the blonde Sierra had trailed to the back of Tony's Tavern in Dusty Lake, New Jersey. Natalia Bonaparte, the article reported, was wanted for questioning in the murder of Giselle Montgomery. Police had found Natalia missing and her apartment ransacked.

How in the world did these two women tie in together?

And look at poor old Yardley, caught in a scandal. She almost felt sorry for him.

She wanted to talk about all of this to someone,

and with a start realized that someone was Pike. How long would that last?

She admitted to herself that she may have panicked and broken it off before she had to. They could have enjoyed each other for another couple of nights before she left for New York and real life inserted itself between them. She closed her eyes, rubbed her forehead and then stood abruptly, strode to the mudroom, grabbed her jacket, stuffed her feet into her ruined boots and marched outside.

The sky was clear, the air cold, the moonlight reflected off the snow. She made her way to the barn, which was now dark, found a lantern and turned it on. The three dogs ambled out of one of the open stalls and stared at her. The place was still set up for the wedding, and she stood there for a second recalling the touching ceremony she'd witnessed.

To be honest, she'd watched Pike more than the wedding couple. He'd looked so sexy in that suit, so sure of himself, so independent. Frankie and Chance had joined him after the ceremony and she'd watched their fond interaction with a touch of envy. She'd told Pike once that he was easy to love.

She suspected that she was not.

A horse whinnied in a nearby stall and she and the dogs approached it to find the same mare she'd ridden to the mine two nights before. The big animal nuzzled her neck then bumped her cheek with a soft, velvet nose.

Sierra stared into the mare's big eyes. "Are you antsy, too, girl? Looking for some action? I know how you feel. Now, if you and me were in New York, we could clip-clop down to the diner no matter what time of day or night and gab with the night shift. You'd like Billy. He wears a bolo tie, very Western. Or maybe we could go to a bar. I could use a glass of wine. What do horses drink? Water? Yeah, we could get me a nice pinot gris and you an icy trough of Perrier with a slice of lemon. But here we are in Idaho." She looked down at the three dogs, who were leaning against her legs. "What the heck do you guys do in the middle of the night when you're restless?"

One dog whined, one yawned and one cocked his ears as the mare blew hot air on Sierra's hair.

Sometimes it didn't pay to think things through. Sometimes, a person just had to rely on their gut or whatever it was that propelled action, no matter how ill-advised.

She quickly saddled the horse, doused the lantern and led the beast outside. Once astride, she took off on a moonlight ride. She'd only been to her current destination one time before, but she was pretty sure she knew how to find her way.

PIKE OPENED THE door on the first knock.

Some part of him had known it would be Sierra.

"Is something wrong?" he asked. It was a natural question given the past several days. Her cheeks were pink and her teeth clattered together.

"No, no. I put my horse in your barn. I hope that's okay."

"You rode over here?"

She nodded. "I saw your lights on—"

"What are you doing here?" he interrupted. She bit her lip. More than anything in the world he wanted to usher her inside, but not until he understood what her presence meant.

"I was wrong," she said, darting a glance up to his eyes. "I don't want it to end like this. I don't know, I think I got scared. I think I started worrying that I was getting in over my head and that you and I—"

He took a step outside to cup her face and draw her to him. He kissed her into silence and then he kissed her again. She grabbed his shirt at the shoulders and pulled him closer. For a moment it was LA revisited, the sensation of her body pressed into his, the sweet smell of her skin, heated desire overwhelming everything.

"Come inside," he finally said, and pulled her though the door, where he wrapped his arms around her and kissed her again and again.

She finally pushed him away. Her lips were hot now, her eyes filled with the same lust that swelled in his body. And then she said, "What's that noise?" and reality flooded back.

He stepped aside to reveal Daisy lying on her dog bed, the proud mother of nine tiny, snuffling, mostly yellow puppies, although there were a couple of brown ones, as well. Sinbad had flown up to the mantel when Sierra knocked and now surveyed the proceedings with his superior yellow gaze.

"Oh, my gosh," she said. "When did this happen?"

"During the wedding. Daisy had to usher her family into the world all by herself."

"Maybe Sinbad offered emotional support," Sierra said.

He smiled. "Somehow I doubt it."

Sierra released his hand and walked over to sit down next to the dog bed. "Look at you with your babies," she said to Daisy, who appeared a tad bewildered. Sierra touched one tiny ear with the tip of her finger. "So soft!"

"Go ahead, pick one up," Pike said as he kneeled beside her and rested his butt on his heels.

"They're too tiny! I might hurt it."

"You won't hurt it," he said gently.

She carefully lifted the plump puppy with both hands and cuddled it against her chest, under her chin. "It's so sweet, Pike," she said and her voice held a note of tenderness that raced through his veins like a shot of whiskey. Daisy's ears perked up when Sierra put the baby back where she'd found it. The dog immediately began licking away all the human cooties.

"I was just about to go to bed," Pike said, curling a tendril of Sierra's hair around his finger. "It's been an awfully long day."

"May I stay here for the rest of the night?" she asked, looking up at him.

"It depends. Where do you want to sleep?"

"With you," she said. "I want to sleep in your bed with you."

He stood, then reached down and grabbed her hands, pulling her to her feet. He slowly lowered the zipper on her jacket and peeled it away from her sweater, dropping it onto an armchair, then he lifted her into his arms. The master bedroom was at the far end of the barn, a huge room filled with his grandmother's antique furniture. He set her down in front of the four-poster bed.

"We didn't turn off the house lights," she said, gesturing toward the hall.

"To hell with the lights." He pulled her sweater over her head and discovered she hadn't worn a bra. The sight of her beautiful skin and the perfect globes of her breasts shot heat into his groin. "Let them burn all night," he whispered as he lowered his head to taste each pebble-hard nipple.

SIERRA'S RINGING PHONE woke her the next morning and she sat up straight like a shot, yanked from yet another bizarre dream. It was still dark outside, but a houseful of lights shone through the open door into the bedroom, and she dug her phone from the pile of discarded clothes on the floor.

"Hello?"

"It's me," Tess said. "I saw that you texted in the middle of the night on Pike's phone. Where are you?"

"I didn't want you to…uh, worry about me," Sierra stammered. It was cold standing naked outside the covers. "I'm at Pike's house. His dog had puppies and I wanted, well, to see them."

"Oh," Tess said, and if she saw through the flimsy lie, she kept it to herself. "Well, Dad says to tell you we're leaving in one hour."

"I'll be there."

She clicked off the phone and prepared to turn to face the bed, but before she could move, Pike grasped her from behind and tugged her back under the blankets. Both of them laughed until the blazing awareness that flared between them stole the smiles away.

"I have to get back to the ranch house," she said as he covered her body with his own. His strong arms pinned her in place and she rubbed her hands over his muscles.

He looked down into her eyes. "Do you have ten minutes to spare?"

"I can give you five," she murmured with a slow smile, distracted by the way their bodies melted together.

"Then we'd better get to it," he said, burying his face in her neck.

PIKE STOOD ON the ranch road and watched Doug's rental turn onto the highway and speed off toward Boise. He thought he saw Sierra wave through the back window, but he wasn't sure. He got back in his truck and headed to the main house.

He'd wanted to drive her to Boise himself, but she'd refused. Better they should say goodbye at the ranch, she insisted, and besides, she had to talk to Tess about Raoul. She had a point.

The best antidote for the uneasiness that just wouldn't go away was work, and that was why he'd made plans with Frankie to help pack up the film crew, who were also leaving today. First he went home, fed Sinbad, checked on Daisy and her brood, saddled Sierra's mare and rode her back to the ranch. When he got there, he found the crew still eating breakfast. He went out to the barn and helped Chance clean up from the night before, until Lily asked him to drive Charlie to his school bus. For a few moments, Pike stood alone.

He and Sierra had made no big promises, no vows of undying love, no plans to ever see each other again, and yet he knew he wouldn't last long before he needed to hold her in his arms. However, there was a very real concern in his heart that she would get home, that her life would consume her and that as the days and weeks passed, she would write him off as a fling she once had with a cowboy.

The crew eventually started hauling their equipment out into the yard. Once again as Pike joked around with them and helped them with their things, he could not wrap his head around one of them feeding information to that disgruntled former employee. He asked a couple of semileading questions as he helped stow their gear, but no one rose to any kind of bait.

After they'd left, it was Pike's turn to drive out to distribute hay to the cattle with Frankie and his dad. By the time he got back to the ranch, the day was getting old and he checked his phone. One text from Sierra since her phone had obviously started working once she got back to "civilization."

Caught an early plane. Thank goodness. Have stop-overs in every little Podunk city between here and home.

Not in the mood for company, he declined dinner at his dad's house and drove home. He hadn't seen Gerard and Kinsey all day—hadn't expected to. This was their honeymoon, after all, or the only one they would get until a break between calving and summer chores would take them to Hawaii for two weeks. He envied them and not just for the warm weather.

The barn was very still. Daisy roused from a nap as he built a fire and contemplated the evening ahead. A knock on the door served as a poignant reminder of a similar knock in the middle of the night, and he opened it with his heart in his throat. Officer Robert Hendricks stood on the threshold.

"Come on in. I'll get you a beer while you admire Daisy's new family," Pike said.

"I'll take water instead," Robert said. "I'm still on duty. Hey, look at all of these cuties. Do you have homes for them yet?"

"Nope."

Pike handed Robert a glass of water and took a swallow from a beer bottle while Robert peered at each of the babies. "Save me one," he said. "The girls have been clamoring for a puppy."

"Maybe you should take two, one for each of them. They'll be ready to go in eight or nine weeks. Bring the kids over anytime to choose which ones they want."

"Deal."

"What do you want to talk about?" Pike asked. "I assume it has something to do with the attack in the mine."

"Yeah. I went by the ranch house hoping to see Sierra Hyde."

"She left this morning."

"That's what I heard. Did she mention we found a matchbook in the mine?"

"From The Pastime on Seventh, right?"

"Wrong. Techs were able to lift the area code from the phone number on the back cover. The place is in New Jersey."

"New Jersey!" Pike said. His throat closed and he set aside the beer.

"It turns out The Pastime is a popular name for a drinking hole. Without the rest of the phone number it leaves three establishments as possibilities."

"Was one in a place called Dusty Lake? Sierra was there recently."

"No." He rattled off three towns Pike had never heard of. "We're looking into it. Should know more tomorrow. I sure would like to speak with Ms. Hyde. Do you expect to talk to her?"

"She's flying standby. She could be anywhere. I'll phone her and leave a message."

"Do you have any idea at all who would wish her harm or who had all that information about her and her sister?" Robert asked.

"None," Pike said. "Did the Seattle police have anything to say about the LOGO crew?"

"Clean as a whistle. The local police apparently

weren't aware the company had a continuing problem with their former employee, who is currently interviewing for a job in Alaska, by the way. It doesn't rule him out entirely, but I have a feeling what happened here is out of his league."

Pike's gut told him the same thing. He shot to his feet and paced up and down the room. He'd told Sierra last night that with Raoul Ruiz off the list of suspects, he thought it possible the attacks had been centered on her. She'd dismissed the whole idea.

What exactly awaited her when she stepped off that plane?

Chapter Twelve

As soon as Sierra hit the influence of the airport cell tower, she found a new string of texts from clients and friends, but nothing from Savannah.

As she waited for a flight, she checked the news on her phone. Yardley had gone on the attack, swearing to anyone who would listen that he was an innocent man being framed by the Jakes camp. He threatened lawsuits. The picture of him this time showed an enraged red face behind a sea of microphones. There were no photographs of the two women.

Sierra had written Pike that her flights were taking her to every pit stop between Boise and New York, but it was actually only three. For the final leg, she had to run between terminals and arrived out of breath. Anxious to relax, all she wanted for the next hour or two was to close her eyes, but her seatmate was a real chatterbox. His only redeeming quality, as far as Sierra was concerned, was his accent. It was pure Jersey shore, and reminded Sierra of Rollo Bean and summers with her father.

After the plane finally landed, she turned her phone

back on to discover that Pike had left her a voice mail. The thrill of hearing his voice was followed by alarm at the urgency of the message. She dialed his number while the plane still taxied down the runway. "Sierra, Robert—Officer Hendricks came by. The matchbook from The Pastime is from New Jersey!"

"Where in New Jersey?"

He told her the three towns.

"They're close to Dusty Lake but I've never been in any of them," she said.

"He'll keep me updated and I'll get back to you."

"Try not to worry about me, okay?" she said.

"I'm afraid worrying comes with caring," he replied as they hung up. By now, she longed for the peace and quiet of her own four walls, where she'd installed the requisite two locks on her door and bars on her windows.

She caught a cab and gave her home address. The driver was from Bangladesh; his English was minimal, but his musical voice fascinated her. What was with her and accents lately? She'd always liked them, had always been good with voices. That's why Spiro's spoken demand to the bartender that night had surprised her, or maybe more accurately, that's why learning he could turn off his Greek accent, and do it so completely, came as a shock. In her experience people had trouble doing that. On the other hand, Savannah said he was an actor.

She warily let herself into the locked lobby of her apartment building, looking around for ne'er-do-wells with murderous intent. The only ones in attendance were the two candidates for mayor in the form of campaign posters plastered to the foyer's walls. Someone had drawn a mustache on Max Jakes's face and someone else had sketched devil horns and a pitchfork on Yardley's leering visage.

She pulled the suitcase up two flights of stairs instead of taking the elevator, because it had a habit of stalling and she wasn't in the mood. The familiar sounds of crying babies and televisions came from behind her neighbors' closed doors. She'd been looking forward to returning to her real life, and here she was and it all fell kind of flat.

But that was because Pike wasn't here and suddenly she understood he would never fit into this world; he could never be more than a visitor. What would he do in an apartment? Where would he put his horses and his dogs and that impossible cat? The man was busy just about every minute of the day and from what she could see, every day of the year. She'd never even seen him watch television or check email. City life would never suit him.

She unlocked her door at last. The relief at being safely home disappeared when she switched on the lights and saw the mayhem her apartment had become in her absence. For a second she just stood in the open doorway and stared at the mess. She examined the locks: they looked perfect... This B&E was the work of a pro.

It didn't appear the intruder had overlooked one item in his or her search for...well, for what? She didn't have expensive art or jewelry. Her television was so old her friends made fun of it. The only thing she had that was worth money was in her head, the gun cabinet or on her computer...

Stepping over and around overturned boxes and emptied drawers, she hurried to her office. Her dad's big, old, wood desk sat where it always did, but the desktop computer was gone and the file drawers were empty. She stood there with her heart in her stomach. Almost everything on the desktop was also on her laptop. It wasn't that she'd lost much besides sentimental files she hadn't transferred, but the scope of the information about herself and her clients the robber now possessed made her queasy.

And the email. Every communication she'd sent or received not only recently, but also going back years, was accessible on that computer. Luckily she used passwords. The opened drawers and ripped books instantly chided her smugness—why else had the thief ransacked things if not to find the passwords? She made her way to her bedroom, intent on pulling the double bed away from the wall and securing the envelope of passwords she'd taped to the wood frame. The bed was already moved aside and the envelope was gone.

Even without the passwords, someone with enough expertise could get what they wanted, but with them it wouldn't even be a tactical feat. And that meant, depending on when this robbery took place, someone knew about Tess and Danny and all the rest.

And Savannah. Face it, Savannah's quietness nagged at her. After checking to make sure the revolver was still where it belonged in the gun case, she opened her laptop and plugged it in, then looked up Savannah on the search engine. There was a recent photo taken of her at a theater opening and a couple as a former Miss Georgia. Her life was summed up in a couple of paragraphs. There was also a link to Spiro Papadakis, the man Savannah had married, and Sierra went to that.

She hadn't realized he'd been such a successful businessman in Greece. She guessed she'd just assumed Savannah had all the money. Then she read that he lost everything and soon after married Savannah and it began to make sense. There were all sorts of further links, but there was absolutely no mention of him being an actor in any capacity. Even his time in New York as a relative nobody was detailed, but again, no mention of acting.

Something didn't add up.

After reporting the break-in to the police, she found the TV remote on the floor among the scattered contents of an upended box of memorabilia. She sat wearily on the sofa, flipped on the television and turned down the volume as she began recollecting the bits and pieces of her dad's campaign souvenirs littered around her feet.

A flyer from 1999 had been crumpled beyond repair, but she did find the big button imprinted with his smiling face and the words "Jeremy Hyde for Mayor." She put that back with a few of his books; he'd been partial to Robert Service poetry. There were several loose photographs scattered about, as well. She was in a couple, either with her dad or sitting at a table stacked with posters. Rollo Bean and her dad were in another. She'd forgotten how tall and straight her dad stood and how overweight Rollo was. There were other differences, too—some obvious, like Rollo's baldness and her dad's thatch of graying black hair, and others internal. Her dad was a peaceful, listening man who cared about people as people. Rollo was a plotter, a born politician.

As she started to set aside the photo, she caught a glimpse of a ten- or twelve-year-old boy standing by a tree behind the two men. It appeared he was eavesdropping. She looked closer and smiled to herself as she recognized Rollo's son, Anthony, who was doing exactly what she'd told Pike he did. There he was, caught on film being, well, creepy.

The past kept surfacing in the form of a half-dozen small items that brought back memories: a menu from Jersey Dog, another from Bee's Fish and Chips, a pennant from the Dusty Lake Bullfrog Labor Day Race and a paper coaster embossed with a line drawing of a building. With some surprise, she realized she'd seen this building recently. The big fish over the door gave it away. She knew it as Tony's Tavern, but The Pastime was printed on the coaster.

Tony's Tavern must have once been called The Pastime!

The apartment buzzer jerked her from her thoughts. She glanced at the television as she stood in time to see a man pop up on the screen. Ralph Yardley, coming out of a hotel, shading his face from the cameras. Things looked to be sliding downhill for him.

Two officers buzzed from downstairs and seconds later knocked on her door. She was stunned they'd actually reacted this quickly and invited them inside, where they shook their heads as they perused the mess. As one grabbed a notepad from his pocket to take information, the other gazed at the television.

"Can you believe that?" he said, elbowing his partner. "I arrested that gal once for soliciting. Who knew she was the Broadway Madame?"

Sierra looked at the screen. The footage of Ralph Yardley was over and now there was a still photo of Natalia Bonaparte. "Wait a second," she said. "The woman on the television right now is *the* Broadway Madame? Are you positive?"

"Yeah. It's all over the news. Apparently the murdered girl, the one who was drowned in a bathtub or something—"

"Not the river?"

"No, that just came out a few hours ago. The water in her lungs did not come out of the Hudson. Anyway, she called Bonaparte the night she died. Police went to Bonaparte's apartment to talk to her and found that she was missing."

"I knew most of that. How did they decide she was the Madame?"

"They came across a secret book filled with women's names and a code. Who knew people write things down nowadays? Giselle Montgomery was on the list along with a bunch of other girls."

"And all of it seems linked back to Ralph Yardley," the other policeman said. "Whether or not he has anything to do with what's going on, that guy's goose is cooked. I bet the Jakes camp is as happy as a bushel of clams at high water."

"Max Jakes strikes me as someone who'd rather win on his own merit than because of something like this," Sierra said softly.

One cop opened his mouth, looked at his partner and shut it without speaking. He looked around the apartment and cleared his throat. "About your problem. Tell us what's missing. Do you know when the break-in occurred?"

Sierra sat down because her knees felt weak. The state of her apartment seemed secondary to everything else swirling around in her head. Why was she increasingly sure Natalia and Giselle's fates were linked with hers? She answered the police questions woodenly, so preoccupied she couldn't think straight, relieved when they left. Damn it, she wished Pike was here to help her sort through all of this or maybe hold her tight and make the cold sweat go away. She'd missed him since the moment she left the ranch— him, Daisy and her puppies, the mare and those three silly dogs. Even Sinbad.

Angry at her scattered thoughts and growing sense of uneasiness, she went to work putting things back in drawers and on shelves, then pushing her bed against the wall. Eventually, she collapsed in front of the TV. Somewhere during a lengthy weather report, she fell asleep and didn't rouse until a pounding at the door awakened her.

And thank goodness it did because she'd had another dream featuring bald men. This time she was tied naked to a chair and four of them stood around throwing lit matches at her.

Honestly, this was getting old.

She looked out the peephole before opening the door and found a big man wearing a blue jacket stretched tight over beefy shoulders. He also wore a cap with a black visor pulled low on his forehead. A bushy mustache occupied half his lower face.

"Yes?" she asked.

"Delivery," he said, holding up a large cardboard-like envelope.

"What is it?" she called. He hadn't buzzed from downstairs, but that wasn't terribly unusual. People often held doors for each other or buzzed someone with a good story inside.

"I don't know, lady. It's from Internal Revenue. Come on, I ain't got all day."

"Put it in my mailbox in the foyer."

"It's too big for that. Anyway, it says here you have to sign for it."

"I'm not opening the door," she said. "Stuff it in the mailbox or tell me where I can go to pick it up."

"I don't have time for this," he said as her door rattled and the knob turned.

What was he doing? "Go away," she yelled.

The door rattled louder. Apparently, the delivery-man's antics drew attention because she heard locks sliding and then the voice of the fireman who lived across the hall. "Dude, quiet down," he called. "I got a kid asleep in here."

The deliveryman told him what he could do with his sleeping child. She peered through the peephole, but she couldn't see anyone. She ran across her apartment and pushed aside the drapes. Her living room window looked out on the street, and she waited for a minute until a man came out of the building. He turned to look up and she stepped back but kept watching. He spoke into a cell phone as he stood on the curb with the big envelope still in his hand. Within seconds, a long white car rolled to a stop on the street in front of him and he slid into the passenger seat and drove away.

That was no deliveryman. For the first time in her life, she was afraid of being alone in her own home.

"Think," she told herself.

Okay, there had been way too many bald men in her dreams lately. The only hairless man she'd had any meaningful experience with in her life was Rollo Bean. She hadn't seen him in almost fifteen years, so what did he represent to her? The past, obviously. Her dad. Elections. New Jersey.

And what about The Pastime? Did that bar have any significance? She'd probably seen it as a child, but if it had always been a drinking establishment, she might not have actually gone inside. But then she recalled the feeling of déjà vu she'd experienced sitting at the mahogany bar that night... She'd attributed it to the fact that many bars looked alike.

Who would know? Who could help? There was only one person she could think of and that was Rollo Bean. Where was he now? How could she find him? She opened her laptop, but the first thing she did was write another email to Savannah asking for details about Spiro's acting experience. To her utter amazement, Savannah wrote back at once. There's quite a bit to say, she said. Come to my place in an hour. Now that you're back in the city, we need to plan what to do next.

Sierra responded positively, adding a warning to be cautious until she arrived. Finally, she could start getting answers, but first she took the time to change important passwords.

Next she searched for and found Rollo Bean's contact information. She doubted she'd be able to get straight through to him but she tried, anyway. Sure enough, her call went to voice mail and she left a message and went to wash up before leaving for Savannah's.

Her cell phone rang as she ran a comb through her hair. The number was unfamiliar. "Hello?"

"Is this Sierra Hyde?"

"Yes."

"Sierra, this is Rollo Bean. You just called me on the other line. My goodness, it's been years!"

"I know. Thanks for returning the call so promptly."

"No problem. What can I do for you?"

"I have some puzzling questions about a bar that used to be called The Pastime in Dusty Lake. Do you remember it?"

"Yes, sure."

"Do you know if I was ever in the place?"

"Maybe. They served food so it was okay for minors to sit at a booth with an adult. You're not going to believe this, but these days I live very close to there. It's called Tony's Tavern now."

"How long has it had that name?"

"It changed hands a few months ago. Why?"

"It's complicated," Sierra said. That's why the dropped matchbook still had The Pastime printed on the cover. "Rollo, may I drive out to Jersey and pay you a visit? There are some questions—"

"Of course you can," he interrupted. "I'm on my way home right now. Gave a speech out of town last night. I don't know if you're aware of this, but I'm involved in Max Jakes's bid for mayor of New York."

"But surely those people don't vote for the mayor in New York City," she said.

"True, but they do vote for governor of the state and that's where Max is headed next."

"Wow, Rollo, that's the big-time."

"I know. It's been a long time coming."

She paused for a second before adding, "I hate to be a pest, but is there any possibility I could see you today?"

He paused for a second. "My schedule is pretty tight. Heck, who am I kidding? I can't say no to Jeremy Hyde's daughter. I could fit you in, say in an hour or so?"

"Great," she said. "I'll be there."

"Why don't you meet me in Tony's parking lot?" he added. "It'll save you trying to find my place."

"Okay."

"Gosh, I miss your dad."

"I know, so do I," Sierra said. "Can't wait to see you."

"Me, too, kiddo."

She'd no sooner clicked off the phone than it rang again. "Sierra?"

"Pike? Oh, man, is it great to hear your voice. How are Daisy and her babies? Are you just getting up?"

"Not exactly. I've been traveling all night. I just landed in New York."

"You're here?"

"I'm here. I'm in the process of renting a car. Give me your address, honey."

"Pike, you'll never be able to find parking here, you should just take a cab."

"Don't worry about it, I'll figure it out. Just give me your address."

She gave him her address but had to add that she was literally on her way out the door.

"That's okay," he said. "I'll probably get lost a time or two. I'll catch up with you when you get back from wherever you're going."

"But what will you do while I'm gone?"

"I'll figure it out, don't worry. Where are you going?"

"I'm going to meet my father's old friend at Tony's Tavern and go back to his place for a chat. I'll be honest with you, Pike. My apartment was burglarized while I was away. Then, this morning, a fake deliveryman tried to get me to open the door. There's a dead call girl all over the news because of her possible connection to a guy running for mayor...and then there's a missing woman called the Broadway Madame who is the same woman in those photographs I showed you taken at Tony's Tavern, which, get this, used to be called The Pastime. I'm not sure about Savannah... Oh, drat! I forgot all about her."

"What about her?"

"I made arrangements this morning to talk to her about her husband. Frankly, I just want to make sure she's okay. She kind of disappeared for a while and I'm worried."

"Where were you going to meet?"

"At her place."

"Do you want me to go and make sure she's all right?"

"Would you really be willing to do that?"

"Why not. Where does she live?"

She gave him Savannah's address. "Confirm that Spiro was really an actor. Ask her where he was on stage," she added.

"Okay."

"I wish I had the time to wait for you."

"I wish you did, too. I don't like you going out there alone."

"I know, but it's what I do."

"You'll take a gun?"

"Pike, it's early. The tavern won't even be open for regular business."

"Take a gun."

"Okay."

"Seriously, sweetheart. My gut tells me you're in danger. Don't forget what happened in Idaho, okay?"

"I haven't."

"Sierra, I want you to know that I love you. That's why I'm here."

His comment on top of the past hour of overload jolted her. She mumbled something in response and disconnected. Her heart pounded in her chest.

He loved her? Why hadn't she said it back? Because she didn't love him? Because she didn't know if she did or not?

Was that true?

Face it: she wasn't sure about anything.

WELL, PIKE THOUGHT to himself as he navigated the traffic out of LaGuardia, *you aren't in Idaho anymore, that's for sure*. His beloved open fields dotted with cattle had been replaced by miles of blacktop crowded with every kind of vehicle imaginable. After a few minutes, he detected a certain rhythm to the flow and eased into it himself.

Could he live here? Sure, if that's what it took. He had a degree in agriculture. Maybe he could teach. Everyone always teased him that he looked and sounded like a professor. Maybe they had the right idea.

It didn't matter what he did to earn a living. They could visit the ranch for vacations. All that mattered was that Sierra and he were together. She might not have been able to say she loved him when he blurted it out, but he knew in his heart that she cared and that was good enough for now.

It was important to keep his mind on the road, but it was impossible not to worry about what was going on with her. He couldn't shake the fact that she was in danger but he couldn't imagine why. What did she have to do with dead and missing women and politicians, and what was with the delivery guy?

Eventually, he found Savannah Papadakis's building a few blocks from Central Park. He pulled up to the curb in front as a doorman immediately shot through the doors and waved his arms. "Sorry, sir, you can't park here," he said.

"Do you have visitor parking? I don't think I'll be long. I'm here to see Savannah Papadakis."

"She's not here."

"When will she be back?"

The doorman looked around as though to make sure no one was listening to him. "We're not sure. See, her hubby moved out a while ago. Mrs. Papadakis is kind of a quiet lady, doesn't socialize very much anymore. But a few days ago, a deliveryman shows up here with an envelope from her husband's attorney."

"What did this guy look like? What company did he work for?"

"I'm not sure. Big bushy mustache, wonky eyes, blue uniform."

"Wonky eyes? What does that mean?"

"They was two different colors. Brown and gray. Made it look like he was staring at you and the guy standing next to you at the same time. Anyway, I called Mrs. Papadakis and she said to send him up. Then she calls down for her car, a big old Cadillac she hardly ever drives, and they both take off, her in that red cape she wears like Little Red Riding Hood."

"Did she say where they were going?"

"Neither one of them said a word."

"Did she have a suitcase?"

"Yeah."

"Did you check her apartment when she didn't come home?"

"The manager did. Everything looked fine."

"Have you since called the police?" Pike persisted.

"Why? It ain't illegal to take a trip. She's a private kind of woman and she's rich. You don't mess with her type."

"So, she's been gone several days with no explanation. You need to take a chance of annoying her and tell someone. At least call her husband."

"She'll kill me if I call her husband."

"Then call the police. Something is wrong." He took a card out of his wallet. It showed green pastures and cattle. Pike's name and phone number occupied one corner while the other said: Hastings Ridge Ranch, Falls Ridge, Idaho. "Tell them to talk to me."

"Idaho?"

"Just do it."

He eased back into traffic and drove until he found a place he could pull over for a minute. He grabbed his phone and called Sierra, alarmed when she didn't respond. By now, he'd been driving around

New York for ninety minutes; surely she'd had time to reach her destination and could answer a phone call. Even if she was still driving she would have put him on speaker.

Maybe reception was bad at Rollo Bean's house. *Think*.

Sierra had been robbed. She said they took her computer. If the mail on all her gadgets was connected like his were, that meant every message she sent and received was visible to the thief and that meant this person would know a whole bunch about her movements.

Grace had mentioned seeing a map of Hastings Ridge Ranch on Sierra's phone. If she'd taken the picture with her phone and sent it to her laptop, then it would have been on her desktop as well and that meant the people in the mine could have known of its location by studying the map. They would also know whatever Tess and Sierra wrote to each other while they were in LA. That meant they knew that there was a question about Danny being dead or alive, but not that his body had actually been found.

And they'd know all about Savannah Papadakis.

All along, it had worried him that the attackers didn't kill Sierra and Tess outright. He'd seen no point in trying to stage an accident instead of getting the job done unless the point was that no one dig into possible motives for murder.

What else was on Sierra's computer? All her work-related information, including the pictures she'd taken with her eyeglass camera at the bar in Jersey—the bar she was headed to right now, the one that used to be called The Pastime, the place the matchbook in the cave had to have come from. And she was on her way to meet Rollo Bean, her dad's old advisor, the man who had fathered a calculating kid with different-colored eyes.

Too many coincidences; too many questions. He programmed his phone to find out how to get where he was headed and pulled back onto the street, his jaw set, his mind focused. Logic said they'd pass each other without even knowing it. His gut told him to go, anyway.

The car was a hell of a lot faster than a horse, but he sure wished he had a shotgun and a better idea of what he would find when he got there.

And he hoped against hope that he wasn't too late.

Chapter Thirteen

Sierra hadn't spent much time in Dusty Lake since her father died. Rollo Bean had been out of the country and unable to come to the funeral so it had been even longer since she'd seen him.

Her dad had loved it here, had hoped to become the town's mayor, but that hadn't worked out. The race seemed to sour him on politics and he took up fishing when he lost the election. He'd told her the week before he died that he wished he'd figured out fishing beat politics all to hell a lot earlier in his life.

This far into the winter, the tree branches were bare and ice shimmered on the lake surface. The skies were as gray as the water and laced with threatening clouds promising showers. She parked next to a large white car sporting two Maxwell Jakes for NYC Mayor bumper stickers and assumed it belonged to Rollo Bean. He wasn't in the car. There was a van parked next to that and a big truck across the lot. The sign hanging under the painted fish over the door said Closed, but that was about the only other place to look. As she approached, the door opened and a man stepped out.

"Sierra Hyde, you haven't changed a bit," he called.

Her mouth almost dropped open. "Rollo?"

"Rolland now, please. Tony came in early, saw me sitting out there in my car and insisted I come in out of the cold." He glanced at his watch and added, "I'm running late so let's just talk here, okay?"

"Sure," she said and brushed past him as she entered the tavern. It was hard to reconcile this trim man with the chubby Rollo Bean she'd known as a kid; he'd lost about half his body mass. "You look very dapper," she said when they faced each other. He wore a crisp white shirt and a black vest with a blue tie. A gold watch sparkled on his wrist.

"Your dad gave me this watch," Rollo said when he saw what had caught her attention. "Do you remember it?"

"No," she said. "I don't. It's very attractive."

"And distinctive," he said, pointing out the four rubies set into the face, one at each quarter hour. "I thought for sure you'd recall it when you saw it. Come sit down. I took the liberty of ordering something hot to chase away the chill."

He led her back to a table across from the booth Natalia and the man who looked like Spiro Papadakis had occupied a week before.

So much had happened in such a short time.

Rollo—she just could not think of him as Rolland— poured them each a mug of coffee from the gold carafe sitting on the table. He took a sip of his and emitted a satisfied sigh. "I'm glad you called me," he said. "I've heard you're working as a PI now."

She was surprised that he'd kept up with her career. "Yes," she said.

"Do you remember the time I brought a lady friend to your father's place? She said she was from France, do you recall? But you told me privately that you thought she was from Quebec. There was something about her accent, you said."

"I was just a kid," Sierra said. "Apparently kind of an obnoxious one."

"On the contrary. You were absolutely right about her. You have a knack for accents and voices, don't you?"

Her brow wrinkled. As a matter of fact, she did, but what was this all about?

"Like my Jersey accent, right? It's distinctive and regional. Like my son's."

"I suppose," Sierra said.

"Combine that with a naturally curious mind and, well, I can see why you're successful at your craft. Now, what exactly is bothering you?"

Quite a lot is bothering me, Sierra thought as she bought thinking time with another swallow of coffee. Things like the feel inside this tavern and Rollo's out-of-context comments that nevertheless were right on point. There was a shrewd look in his eyes as he stared at her, a familiar look that made her wish she'd waited for Pike. It also telegraphed caution.

"You look confused," he said.

She sipped again and wondered if she had the audacity to just get up and leave.

"About that curiosity factor of yours," he said when she remained seated and thoughtful. "Did I mention that besides having my stomach stapled and plastic surgery on my nose and chin I also bought a fantastic wig straight from Paris? Do you wonder what I look like in it?"

Not really, she thought, but managed to mumble, "I'm sure…you…look great." The warmth from the coffee sliding down her throat felt good in part because her head had started to swim. And then her thoughts flashed back to the old gold mine. The men were talking to each other. They had Jersey accents, just like Rollo's. That's what had been bugging her.

She blinked as she met his gaze. She was in trouble and she knew it, but she wasn't a hundred percent sure why. Her gun was in her purse, which was hanging by its strap from the back of her chair. "What's going…on?" she said, alarmed at how difficult it was to speak. She looked at the cup in her hand and then at his. He took a healthy swallow… Had he put something in her mug before he poured her coffee? "You're…Dad's…friend."

"Friend? No, there are no friends in politics. Frankly, it was a relief when he quit. He didn't have the stomach for it. I'm on to bigger and better things and nothing, or no one, is going to ruin it. Now, about my new look. Let me satisfy your curiosity." He opened a box that sat on the chair beside him and took out an expensive-looking wig of shiny white hair. He pulled it over his head, adjusted it quickly and peered at her. "Did I get it on straight? I'm used to a mirror. Okay, what do you think? Do I look distinguished?"

She stared at him with wide eyes. His surface resemblance to Spiro Papadakis was nothing short of amazing. Maybe their mothers could have told them apart, but in a bar at night—it could throw anyone off.

Did this mean Savannah's friend had seen Rollo in this bar and jumped to the conclusion it was Spiro? Was the whole thing nothing more than a giant mistake? But wait, if it was Rollo, then he'd been sitting here with Natalia right before she disappeared.

All those dreams about bald men taunting her, tackling her, calling her an idiot—had she somehow recognized Rollo despite the changes to his appearance?

Sierra put the cup of coffee down too hard and it slopped onto her hands. Rollo shoved a napkin toward her and she stared at it, unable to make sense of what was happening. Her eyelids drooped; her muscles felt spongy. The gun might as well be hanging from the Statue of Liberty's upraised torch.

She looked at the coffee staining her fingers then back at Rollo. He had two faces now and she internally groaned. "You—you..." she sputtered but the rest of the words wouldn't come.

He lowered his voice and leaned toward her. "The minute I saw you wearing those photo glasses, I knew you were up to no good, and what else could it be but to catch me with Natalia? That was bad enough, but later that night when the other whore…died…well, your fate was sealed. When I found out you were leaving town, I stole your computer. Isn't the information age grand? Your whole life, the past, the present, right there before me and actually moving forward as you scurried around like a busy mouse telling all your buddies every little detail of everything you saw and thought and did. I deduced from all your communications that you didn't know it was me in here that night, but I also knew you had questions and that meant you'd keep digging and eventually you'd put two and two together. And if you ever wised up and looked closer at the watch, I was dead meat.

"Tony and his stupid idiot pal were supposed to get rid of you in Idaho, but Sierra, dear, you're like a cockroach! Then this morning you wouldn't open your door to let him in. And just when I was trying to figure out what to do next, you announce you're going to the Papadakis apartment. I responded to you by using Savannah's tablet. It wasn't a perfect solution, but I thought I could work with it. And then, you actually call me! What a lovely turn of events. The fly came to the spider."

Another man walked up to the table. This one was a bulky, clumsy-looking guy about Sierra's age, meaty through the shoulders in a too-tight plaid shirt. The flagrant mustache was gone, but she knew she'd seen him last in front of her apartment talking on his phone. The white car in the parking lot—Rollo's car—must have been the vehicle that picked him up.

The man smiled as he gazed down at her and she cringed. Those eyes. Anthony. Tony.

"Welcome to my tavern, Sierra. Sorry the coffee… disagreed with you."

That voice! She pushed herself away from the table and tried to stand, but her knees started to buckle. She grabbed for her purse and missed it. Anthony hoisted her to her feet and flung her across one shoulder.

Her head just about exploded against his back. "You know where to put her. We'll take care of… disposal…later."

"How?"

"I don't know yet. Just get her car out of the parking lot in case someone comes looking."

Sierra was conscious of being carried across the room, her dangling hands hitting the backs of chairs. She blacked out for a while and came to when she landed on a hard, cold surface. She had somehow acquired tape around her ankles and hands, and a gag in her mouth. Her eyes sprang open. Another woman lay beside her. Natalia!

And then a loud rattling noise heralded darkness and a welcome return to oblivion.

Pike pulled into Tony's Tavern. The place had a Closed sign on the door even though it was almost four o'clock in the afternoon. He'd hit a bad accident halfway between New York and here and had been held up for what seemed like forever. He'd called the Dusty Lake police as he waited for traffic to clear and asked them to check out the tavern and Rollo Bean's residence. They hadn't sounded real motivated but someone had eventually called him back and told him there was a sign on the tavern saying it was closed due to illness and no one named Rollo Bean lived in or around Dusty Lake.

While he'd waited for the police to call him back, he'd looked up Rollo Bean's number and called him, too. No answer. Where in the hell was everybody? Now he tried one last time to contact Sierra, grimacing when the phone switched directly to messages.

What did he do now?

He got out of the rental, grateful to stand after hours of sitting. There were two other vehicles in the parking lot, a newish gray van and a large white truck, both with New Jersey plates, which meant Sierra's car wasn't here. As he walked by the van, he checked the interior through the window and saw fast food wrappers and a clipboard. No sign of Sierra.

He walked over to the box truck. It appeared to be about fifteen feet long and had seen better days. Pike wouldn't want to take it out on the interstate. It was also outfitted with refrigeration. The low hum of a compressor kicked on as he examined the solid lock on the rear door. He continued on to the tavern, read the sign the police had mentioned and knocked loudly, surprised when the door actually opened and a man appeared.

He was a big guy in his thirties and he looked a little sweaty despite the cold. He wore a green plaid shirt buttoned all the way up to the beginnings of a double chin. His hairline had started to retreat up his forehead, emphasizing his eyes. One gray, one brown, both narrowed.

Again the cold hard facts presented themselves: Sierra had come here to meet a friend and that friend had a grown son with different-colored eyes who was now standing in front of him.

Pike's original intention had been to ask around and see if someone had seen Sierra, but now he decided to be more casual about it. This guy had the look and smell of a cornered bull.

"Sorry to bother you," he began with a smile. "I have plans to meet a buddy here for a beer but it looks like you're closed."

"We are," the man said and started to shut the door.

Pike tried stalling. "Can I wait here for my friend?"

"What? No. We're closed."

"How about I buy a beer and wait inside? It looks like it's going to rain."

"What part of closed don't you get?"

"Maybe the owner—"

"I'm the owner and I say get lost." The door slammed and a lock clicked in place.

Okay, so that was Rollo Bean's son. Someone matching his vague description had left with Savannah Papadakis. This was the place Sierra had come to meet Rollo Bean and since announcing that intention, she hadn't responded to any of his calls. He could almost feel her vibes lingering here. He wanted desperately to get inside that bar.

In case he was being watched, he walked back to

the rental and drove out of the lot, pulling in behind an abandoned bait store a half block away. He got out of the car and sprinted back to the tavern, this time approaching from the rear and keeping low. There was a door at the back that was locked, but there was another around the corner next to the garbage cans that was open. He slipped inside the tavern and found himself in an empty kitchen. The place was poorly lit and ominously quiet except for the sound of Anthony speaking on the phone somewhere deeper inside.

Pike had worked in a similar joint during college and could guess the layout of this one. He methodically began searching for some sign of Sierra. She wasn't in the basement, where food was stored, nor was she in the walk-in refrigerator or freezer. He peeked through a window connecting the kitchen to the main room. Anthony held a phone to his face as he paced up and down between tables and chairs. There was no one in there with him.

Pike pulled off his boots and carried them as he made his way down a dark hallway that connected to another, where he discovered the bathrooms. Empty. All this time his heart stayed lodged in his throat because his head kept telling him Anthony was coming apart at the seams, and if Sierra was here, she was probably hurt or dead.

The thought bruised his heart so deeply it made breathing hard, and he pushed it away. He ducked through an open door and found himself in an office lit only with a gooseneck desk lamp. He checked out the closet. When he turned to leave he noticed a strap of black leather jammed in a file drawer built into the desk. He pulled the drawer open.

A woman's handbag had been stuffed inside. Sierra carried one much like it, but so did a million other women. The zipper was open, and using one hand he moved aside the scattered contents until he saw a bright pink wallet. He recognized that immediately. There was no sign of a gun. In the next instant he realized the voice out in the tavern had gone quiet. A creaking floorboard nearby sent his heart into overdrive.

There wasn't time to do more than slide the drawer shut and hide behind the open door. Things were going to go sour fast if the man closed himself in the office.

The room suddenly came alive with the sound of footsteps and heavy breathing. Furniture moved, a chair squeaked. Next came a grunt and a muttered oath. The door suddenly flew away from Pike and his heart leaped into his throat, but Anthony had closed it behind him as he left and now his footsteps receded down the hall. Pike cautiously let out his breath and walked to the desk. The handbag was gone. He quietly turned the handle on the door and peeked into the empty corridor.

A door slammed some distance away and the building instantly took on the silence of abandonment. Pike ran to look out the front window of the tavern and saw Anthony walking toward the big truck, Sierra's handbag in his hand. He unlocked the back of the truck, threw the handbag inside and relocked it. Then he walked to the driver's door and opened the door to the cab.

Pike pulled on his boots and hightailed it back to the kitchen, letting himself out the way he'd come in. He peered around the corner of the building, expecting to see the truck rolling out of the lot, but it hadn't moved at all. His phone was in his hand. He'd get the police onto that truck no matter what he had to tell them, but he wanted a license number. He started circling closer, threading his way through the lakeside trees. It started raining and big, cold drops hit his bare head.

Anthony climbed out of the truck, patted all his pockets and began walking back to the restaurant. He kept his head down as he moved, obviously preoccupied. Pike kept moving so that by the time the guy was back at the tavern, Pike was right next to the truck.

As soon as the door closed behind Anthony, Pike checked the lock on the back. He pounded his fist against the rolling metal door and called Sierra's name. There was no response and no time to think— he had to trust his gut and his gut said that the truck had some connection to Sierra. He ran around to the open driver's door and climbed inside. The engine wasn't running and there wasn't a key in sight. The truck keys and the lock keys must be on separate rings.

The old vehicle had a lot in common with the tank truck back on the ranch. How many times had he and his brothers had to hot-wire that old beast? He reached into his pocket for his multitool and then remembered he hadn't been able to bring it on the plane. A rusty toolbox on the floor yielded a gold mine. First a pair of pliers that he used to unscrew the nut holding the ignition in place. With that gone, he pulled the ignition unit free, found a pocketknife in the toolbox and cut the wires. He chanced a look in the rearview mirror. Anthony was two thirds of the way back across the lot, headed for the truck. Pike touched the wires to each other until he found a spark. The engine turned over with a roar and actually sprang to life. He twisted the wires together and hoped for the best.

Anthony was at the rear of the truck now and he'd produced a handgun. Just as Pike pushed down on the accelerator, he felt the rear of the truck dip and realized Anthony had jumped for the rear bumper. There were grab bars back there; presumably, Anthony was holding on for dear life.

The trick would be to get Anthony off the back of that truck in case he had the guts to shoot out the lock before Pike could prevent it. Toward that goal, he gunned his way through the stop sign at the edge of the parking lot and drove under the branches of a low-hanging tree, hoping Anthony would be pried loose. He checked the mirror. Damn. Anthony did not lie sprawled on the wet pavement behind him. He was still on the truck.

A refrigerated truck. Handy for storing bodies. It was pretty obvious to Pike that Anthony had abducted or coerced Savannah Papadakis out of her apartment. Why, he wasn't sure. But it was tied into Sierra, it had to be.

Again that almost preternatural sensation of her essence attacked his senses. He had to get rid of Anthony, he had to get the truck to safety, he had to see if Sierra was where his gut told him she was and, if so, what condition she was in.

He ran another stop sign a few blocks ahead and breezed through a red light a block after that. The windshield wipers barely kept up with the rain. He sat on his horn and flashed headlights at oncoming vehicles. It was a strange city to him and he had no idea where the police department was. It didn't help that it was getting dark really fast. He wasn't even sure of the exact location of the city center, as he'd followed road signs to get to the lake and they had skirted around business areas. He couldn't possibly free his hands or his attention to check his phone for directions or even to chance making a call. Instead he drove with all the skill he'd learned since the day he turned ten and his father plopped him behind a wheel of a truck much like this one, with blocks tied to the pedals, and told him to follow the tractor around the field while they gathered huge rolls of hay.

Frankie was fond of saying that it always seemed there were too damn many cops in the world. Easy for Frankie to say as he was talking about scuffles, boyhood mischief and eventually more serious events, where the least welcome thing was the sight of a badge. What Pike wouldn't give for a cop right now, and driving as fast as he was, certainly someone would call one in. For heaven's sake, there was a man holding on to the back of a speeding, erratically driven old delivery truck. What did it take to get someone's attention around here?

More horn honking and this time the driver honked back. Good. He flashed lights again, opened the window and waved his arm. All during this crazy drive, he constantly checked the rearview mirror because of Anthony. The guy had to be half limpet to have stayed on with that last turn. He slowed for a sharp right and that's when his headlights flashed on a sign telling him the sheriff's department was one mile up ahead. At that same moment, a siren announced itself from the road behind and Pike glanced in the mirror to see welcome red-and-blue lights in hot pursuit. He made it to the sheriff department's parking lot and slowed to a stop. He opened the door in time to see Anthony run under the lights illuminating the gate with police in pursuit. More police warned Pike to stop where he was and keep his hands visible. As Pike settled both his hands on top of his head, the cops caught up with Anthony and disarmed him.

"He stole my truck. He's a madman," Anthony yelled. "I'm a businessman here in this city. Arrest him. What are you waiting for?" His face was pasty white, his hair and clothes soaked.

Pike opened his mouth. Before a word came out, they heard a banging noise coming from inside the truck and muffled sounds of distress.

"Shoot the locks," someone said.

"No," Pike said. "There might be a woman in there. That man has the keys."

"Unlock the truck, sir," the officer told Anthony, who looked frantically from one unyielding face to another before producing his key ring and throwing it to the pavement. He closed his eyes and bowed his head. The police set to work unlocking the truck as an officer cuffed Pike and led him to the back.

"Please," Pike said as he paused. "My girlfriend… please. I have to see her. I have to know…"

"Someone get a light," the man with the keys yelled and a bevy of flashlights switched on as the truck door rolled up on its chains.

Sierra sat against the side of the truck, gagged, her bound hands holding a chain connected to the wall. She had no weapon but herself. She must have kicked the truck to get their attention. Another woman in considerably worse condition lay beside her, eyes open but unblinking. Blood stained her blond hair. She stared at the lights as though caught in their glare as men jumped into the truck and leaned over her. A third woman cried out from farther forward, deep in the shadows, and Pike saw Sierra's head swivel to see who it was.

She was older than the others by a decade, tied to cleats, sitting on a box, gagged. She was thin to the point of being gaunt and tangled dark hair swept the shoulders of a red cape. Dark eyes flashed in her face.

Sierra's gasp was audible even through her gag, and as soon as it was removed, she whispered, "Savannah?"

"Savannah Papadakis," Pike murmured to the officer by his side. "I think she's been stuck in there for days."

"Who's the blonde on the floor?" the officer asked as the sound of ambulance sirens wailed in the distance. "It looks like she's in pretty bad shape."

"Natalia Bonaparte," Sierra said.

"She's been tortured," the officer leaning down to tend to her muttered. He looked at Sierra. "How about you, miss?"

Sierra shook her head. "I'm fine. Just, please, help me stand.

It killed Pike not to be able to go to her aid, but soon enough she'd been freed from her bindings and helped from the truck. Sierra peered up at the sky for a second, closing her eyes as the rain pelted her face, then she moved toward Pike in slow motion, officers stepping aside as she passed. She stopped right in front of him, raised her arms and wrapped them around his neck. Her lips against his felt like heaven on earth. When she pulled away to gaze at him, he thought there might be tears on her cheeks, but with the rain streaking her face, who knew?

He just knew his eyes were damp and it had nothing to do with the weather.

"I love you," she said, her voice hoarse but fierce. "I miss Daisy. I miss my horse."

He smiled, a little confused. "Your horse? Which horse is that?"

"The red mare. What's her name?"

"Ginger."

"I miss Ginger. Please, please, take me home."

Unable to put his cuffed arms around her, he kissed her forehead and rested his chin on top of her wet head. "I was just about to say the same damn thing to you," he whispered.

Epilogue

Sierra had heard the tape a dozen times but the fear behind the hurried, whispered words still caused a shiver to race through her veins.

"Natalia? Pick up, oh, pick up. It's me, Giselle. Are you there? I'm stuck in Max's suite. He thinks I left, but we were smoking crack and I fell asleep... Anyway, that Rollo guy is here. I heard him and Max laughing about some man they put in prison on false charges... If they know I heard... Please, Natalia, answer the phone. I—" At this point the voice ended. Someone who sounded a lot like Maxwell Jakes swore. Giselle cried out, "No..."

That was it, but that had been enough. Minutes after she called Natalia, Max Jakes had allegedly held her head under water until she was dead, and an hour after that, someone fitting Anthony Bean's description was seen dumping something the size and shape of a human body into the Hudson River. By the next afternoon Rollo Bean had used his informant to plant misleading evidence in the Ralph Yardley camp. And twelve hours later, Natalia Bonaparte threatened to

take the police the tape of the underage call girl she'd
sent to Max Jakes's room a half-dozen times…unless a sizeable hunk of cash found its way into her
offshore bank account. She disappeared soon after.

All three men were now under arrest and Giselle's
voice from beyond the grave had helped make that
possible. And that made Sierra very happy.

But not as happy as sitting on this bench in Central Park with Pike by her side. She rested her head
against his and he kissed her hair. His arm around
her shoulders felt wonderful and safe. He'd been in
New York for three days and this was one of the few
times they'd managed to dodge interviews, questions
and the limelight to find peace without staying inside her apartment. Though it was cold, it felt great
to just be outside and alone.

"I have to leave in another day or two," he told her.

"I know."

"I'll come again."

She looked into his eyes. "I know you will but I
have a question. Do you think I could go back with
you?"

A smile lit up his eyes. "I thought you might have
said that the other night because of everything you'd
just been through. Of course you can. I'd love that."

"I can't stay long," she added. "Savannah is such
a wreck she's asked her husband for a reconciliation.
Why in the world Anthony took her instead of just
bashing her over the head when he stole her tablet
is a mystery. And then there's this case I've been
working on—"

He cut her short by picking up her hand and kissing her fingers. "Sierra? Just stay however long you want. That's all I ask."

They stared at each other for a long moment and then both smiled at the same time. "Okay," she said and looked around at the city skyline she loved, then back into Pike's eyes. It was hard not to wonder if she'd ever have the heart to leave his side...

* * * * *

*Look for Frankie's story, the final book in
Alice Sharpe's* THE BROTHERS OF
HASTINGS RIDGE RANCH *later this year.
You'll find it wherever Harlequin books are sold!*

REQUEST YOUR FREE BOOKS!
2 FREE NOVELS PLUS 2 FREE GIFTS!

HARLEQUIN®

INTRIGUE

BREATHTAKING ROMANTIC SUSPENSE

YES! Please send me 2 FREE Harlequin® Intrigue novels and my 2 FREE gifts (gifts are worth about $10). After receiving them, if I don't wish to receive any more books, I can return the shipping statement marked "cancel." If I don't cancel, I will receive 6 brand-new novels every month and be billed just $4.74 per book in the U.S. or $5.49 per book in Canada. That's a savings of at least 12% off the cover price! It's quite a bargain! Shipping and handling is just 50¢ per book in the U.S. and 75¢ per book in Canada.* I understand that accepting the 2 free books and gifts places me under no obligation to buy anything. I can always return a shipment and cancel at any time. Even if I never buy another book, the two free books and gifts are mine to keep forever.

182/382 HDN GH3D

Name _____ (PLEASE PRINT)

Address _____ Apt. #

City _____ State/Prov. _____ Zip/Postal Code

Signature (if under 18, a parent or guardian must sign)

Mail to the **Reader Service:**
IN U.S.A.: P.O. Box 1867, Buffalo, NY 14240-1867
IN CANADA: P.O. Box 609, Fort Erie, Ontario L2A 5X3
**Are you a subscriber to Harlequin® Intrigue books
and want to receive the larger-print edition?
Call 1-800-873-8635 or visit www.ReaderService.com.**

* Terms and prices subject to change without notice. Prices do not include applicable taxes. Sales tax applicable in N.Y. Canadian residents will be charged applicable taxes. Offer not valid in Quebec. This offer is limited to one order per household. Not valid for current subscribers to Harlequin Intrigue books. All orders subject to credit approval. Credit or debit balances in a customer's account(s) may be offset by any other outstanding balance owed by or to the customer. Please allow 4 to 6 weeks for delivery. Offer available while quantities last.

Your Privacy—The Reader Service is committed to protecting your privacy. Our Privacy Policy is available online at www.ReaderService.com or upon request from the Reader Service.

We make a portion of our mailing list available to reputable third parties that offer products we believe may interest you. If you prefer that we not exchange your name with third parties, or if you wish to clarify or modify your communication preferences, please visit us at www.ReaderService.com/consumerschoice or write to us at Reader Service Preference Service, P.O. Box 9062, Buffalo, NY 14240-9062. Include your complete name and address.

HI15

"Paige?" Jax whispered.

He could have sworn everything stopped. His heartbeat. His breath. Maybe even time. But that standstill didn't last.

Because the person stepped out, not enough for him to fully see her, but Jax knew it was a woman.

"You got my message," she said. "I'm so sorry."

Paige. It was her. In the flesh.

Jax had a thousand emotions hit him at once. Relief. Mercy, there was a ton of relief, but it didn't last but a second or two before the other emotions took over: shock, disbelief and, yeah, anger.

Lots and lots of anger.

"Why?" he managed to say, though he wasn't sure how he could even speak with his throat clamped shut.

Paige cleared her throat, too. "Because it was necessary."

As answers went, it sucked, and he let her know that with the scowl he aimed at her. "Why?" he repeated.

She stepped from the shadows but didn't come closer to him. Still, it was close enough for him to confirm what he already knew.

This was Paige.

She was back from the grave. Or else back from a lie that she'd apparently let him believe.

For a *dead* woman, she didn't look bad, but she had changed. No more blond hair. It was dark brown now and cut short and choppy. She'd also lost some of those curves that'd always caught his eye and every other man's in town.

"I know you have a thousand questions," she said, rubbing her hands along the outside legs of her jeans. She also glanced around. Behind him.

Behind her.

"Just one question. Why the hell did you let me believe you were dead?"

Don't miss SIX-GUN SHOWDOWN
by USA TODAY bestselling author Delores Fossen,
available in August 2016 wherever
Harlequin® Intrigue books and ebooks are sold.

www.Harlequin.com

Reading Has Its Rewards

Earn **FREE BOOKS!**

Register at **Harlequin My Rewards** and submit your Harlequin purchases from wherever you shop to earn points for free books and other exclusive rewards.

Plus submit your purchases from now till May 30th for a chance to win a $500 Visa Card*.

Visit **HarlequinMyRewards.com** today

MYR16R1